THE CLUE IN THE
JEWEL BOX

"STOP THAT FELLOW! DON'T LET HIM GET AWAY!"

The Clue in the Jewel Box   *Frontispiece (Page 144)*

NANCY DREW MYSTERY STORIES

THE CLUE IN THE JEWEL BOX

BY

CAROLYN KEENE

ILLUSTRATED BY

RUSSELL H. TANDY

NEW YORK

GROSSET & DUNLAP

PUBLISHERS

CONTENTS

vi   Contents

THE CLUE IN THE
JEWEL BOX

CHAPTER I

A STOLEN WALLET

"No, a silver pen isn't exactly what I want," Nancy Drew explained patiently to the jewelry salesman in the department store.

The slim, attractive girl waited for the clerk to show her something else. Not discouraged, he reached beneath the counter, bobbing up with a small tissue-wrapped package.

"Now here is something you'll like," he declared confidently. "This handsome jewel box came in only a few hours ago."

Nancy, hopeful of finding a suitable birthday gift for her father, eagerly watched the man unwrap the box. Proudly he displayed a jewel case of intricate design.

"Oh, it *is* lovely!" she exclaimed, her blue eyes lighting. "But I believe my father would prefer something less showy."

"He could use this for jewelry, or put it on his desk," the clerk said persuasively. "This little silver case is a clever imitation of a famous one owned by a ruler in Europe two centuries ago."

At the word "imitation," Nancy's pretty face clouded slightly. She had hoped to give

1

her father something original and unusual, not a gift which might be seen in duplicate in many places.

"Well, I hardly know," she began doubtfully.

"The original box has a strange history," resumed the salesman. Well aware of Nancy's reputation as an amateur detective, he hoped to capture her interest with hints of mystery. "The first owner of it was a king heartily disliked by his subjects. One night he was spirited away, and——"

Nancy heard no more of the romantic tale, for a woman customer, evidently annoyed at the storytelling, tapped on the glass counter.

"Young man," she said impatiently, "will you please wait on me?"

"Oh, do so," Nancy urged politely. "I believe I'll think this over, anyway."

The clerk, disappointed by his failure to make a sale, turned to the other customer. Nancy thanked him and left.

She entered an elevator which took her to the floor where there was a tearoom. Here she was to have luncheon with Bess Marvin and George Fayne, two girls who also lived in River Heights. The latter enjoyed her boyish name. The two, who were cousins, frequently shared Nancy's adventures. They had not arrived, so she seated herself in a comfortable chair of the lounge to wait for them.

"Oh, dear, oh, dear!" murmured a voice almost at her elbow.

Turning her head, Nancy saw that the seat beside her own was occupied by an aristocratic elderly lady in a dark blue silk dress. A half-veil screened a sad, once-beautiful face, but it was the pallor of the creamy skin that held the girl's attention. Obviously, the woman was ill.

"Can I help you?" Nancy asked quickly.

The woman fumbled in a beaded purse, then shakily handed her a card. It bore the name Alexandra, and an address, 47 Downing Street.

"Please take me to my home," she whispered. "I feel so ill."

Nancy hesitated, not because she was unwilling to help, but because for an instant she wondered if she might become the victim of a hoax. Although the stranger used perfect English, she spoke with a slight accent.

Before Nancy could reply, her chums, Bess and George, entered the waiting room. As soon as they heard the woman's request, both girls declared that they would postpone their luncheon.

"We'll help you take Mrs. Alexandra to her home," Bess said at once. "But how shall we get her there? By taxi?"

Nancy nodded as she assisted the elderly lady to her feet. The smile with which she was rewarded immediately erased any doubt in the girl's mind that this person intended to bring any harm to her.

"You will not regret your kindness to me," the woman murmured.

The three girls made slow progress to the

street, encouraging Mrs. Alexandra whenever her strength faltered. Summoning a taxi, they assisted her into it, and gave the Downing Street address to the driver.

"Thank you—thank you," the panting woman murmured, and slumped against the cushions in a faint.

"Get to Downing Street as fast as you can," Nancy instructed the driver.

As the cab sped away, the girls chaffed the stranger's hands and fanned her. On the floor lay the beaded purse from which had tumbled several articles. One of these was a jeweled, monogrammed bottle of smelling salts. Its presence suggested to Nancy that its owner was subject to frequent fainting spells.

"She's coming to now," Bess said a moment later as the woman's eyes fluttered. "As soon as she gets home, she'll be all right."

Relieved, Nancy reached down to pick up the beaded purse and its scattered contents. Almost at her feet lay a gold-framed miniature of a little boy in a sailor suit. She stared at the quaint picture, then turned it over. In the back of the case, under glass, were several locks of hair, held in place with tiny clasps set with rubies.

"This is very unusual," thought Nancy.

She had no opportunity to show the miniature to Bess or George. As the cab drew up in front of a small house, she replaced all the articles in the purse, and turned to assist the elderly passenger.

"Can you walk, if we help you?" she inquired anxiously

"Yes, I think so," the woman murmured.

With Bess and George supporting her on either side, she took a few tottering steps. Nancy paid the cabman, then darted ahead to ring the doorbell. She feared the house might be deserted, but to her relief the door was opened by a middle-aged servant in spotless white cap and apron.

"Oh!" the maid cried when she saw her mistress being half-carried up the walk. "Madame Marie has had another of her spells!"

She opened the door wide, and indicated that the woman was to be laid on a brocade-covered couch in the living room.

"Shall we call a doctor?" George inquired as the servant scurried about in search of medicine and needed articles.

"No, it will not be necessary," the patient whispered, trying to smile. "Anna understands my ailment. She will care for me."

It was true that the maid seemed unusually capable in attending her mistress. With loving hands she made the woman comfortable, and gave her a hot beverage which quickly revived her.

For several minutes Nancy had been noticing the unusual furnishings of the room. On the walls hung several tapestries which seemed too elegant for an ordinary house. There were beautiful pieces of furniture covered with hand-embroidered silks. On a table and a desk

stood rare objects of glass and porcelain.
"This is almost like a museum," thought
Nancy.

One piece completely captured the girl's interest. It was a pink enamel Easter egg which
stood on a tiny gold pedestal. Its rounded cover
was encrusted with delicate gold work.

"Did you ever see anything like it?" Bess
whispered in awe.

Her words were not meant for Mrs. Alexandra, who nevertheless heard them. Raising
herself to a sitting position, she remarked that
the Easter egg was brought to America from
abroad.

"Madame Marie, you must not exert yourself," the servant warned her mistress.

"The attack is passing. I feel quite myself
now. Anna, I must talk to these girls who have
been so kind."

The words, quietly spoken, were regarded by
the maid as an order. Bowing low, she left
the room. Most graciously Mrs. Alexandra
thanked Nancy and her friends for their help,
and carefully wrote their names in an attractive little address book.

Observing their interest in the art objects
about them, the woman pointed out several
which were inside a cabinet. Among these was
a silver box that looked very much like the one
at the jewelry counter in the department store.
Nancy wondered if this might be the original
about which the salesman had spoken. Almost

apologetically, the girl spoke of her search for a distinctive birthday gift for her father.

"Of course, I never could afford anything so rare as these lovely pieces," she concluded with a sigh.

"You might be surprised," returned Mrs. Alexandra, smiling rather mysteriously. "Why not go to my friend, Mr. Faber, who is an antique dealer? Mention that I sent you. I think he will find exactly what you want and at a reasonable price, too."

She summoned Anna, asking for one of the antique dealer's business cards. On it she wrote a message. The girls now bade the woman good-by, fearing that more conversation would tax her strength.

"Wasn't it exciting?" Bess asked as soon as the three friends reached the street. "And didn't you just love Mrs. Alexandra? She's so gracious and charming."

"And her treasures are remarkable," Nancy said in a low voice. "I was especially impressed with the Easter egg."

"Right now I'll take my eggs in omelet form without gold trimmings," chuckled George. "When do we have luncheon?"

"Oh, that appetite of yours!" Nancy teased. "Let's go on to Faber's shop. Perhaps we'll pass a restaurant on the way."

A rather long walk brought the three girls back to the center of the River Heights' business section. Presently they turned down a side street, and Nancy stopped to look again at the card Mrs. Alexandra had given her.

Just then a small, wiry man darted from an alleyway, brushing past the girls. He glanced anxiously over his shoulder, then with short, hurried steps entered a shabby-looking apartment house.

"That fellow acts as if he were running away from someone," Nancy remarked, turning to glance down the street. "A crowd has gathered at the corner, too!"

Retracing their steps, the girls joined the excited group. In the center of the circle stood a young man, angrily accusing a second young man of having picked his pocket.

"That's not so," the other defended himself. "I was walking along the street, minding my own business, when you grabbed me! I never saw your wallet!"

The argument waxed warmer, and a police officer arrived to ask what was wrong. Amid the confusion, Nancy edged closer.

"Excuse me," she said to the policeman. "I saw a young man who looks like this one running up the street."

"There!" cried the alleged culprit triumphantly. "I guess that proves my innocence! I've been mistaken for the real thief."

"Which way did the fellow go?" the policeman asked Nancy.

She directed him to the old, four-story apartment building, and he hurried off. The three girls, the young man whose wallet had been stolen, the accused man, and many curious people followed to see what would happen.

Scarcely had the policeman entered the building than those on the street were startled to see a figure appear on a fire escape above an alley. Light as a cat, the man leaped to the ground, and fled.

"That's the fellow!" cried Nancy.

The heavy-set officer came back and hurtled after the thief, commanding him to halt. Instead, the young man squeezed through a gap between two buildings and vanished.

"Look!" Nancy exclaimed alertly. "He dropped the wallet!"

Whether or not the thief deliberately had thrown away the leather case she could not know. A moment later the policeman rejoined the group and presented the wallet to its owner.

"Sorry I couldn't overtake that fellow," he said regretfully. "I'll make a complete report to Central Station. Your name, please?"

"Francis Baum," the other replied. "Never mind the report. I am satisfied to get my property back."

"Nothing was taken from it?"

The young man carefully examined the contents. Nancy, who stood close beside him, saw part of a business card. Her photographic mind made a note of:

thson

ter St.

"My money is all here," the owner of the wallet assured the policeman. "Thanks for your trouble."

Francis Baum and the man he had accused walked away, the officer went off to make his report, and the crowd dispersed. Bess and George likewise would have gone on had not Nancy held them back.

"Just a minute," she pleaded, starting down the alley. "I want to search the ground between those two buildings."

"You don't think the thief is still there!" George scoffed, following reluctantly.

"No, but I thought I saw something fall from the wallet when it was dropped."

"Wouldn't the policeman have found it?" Bess protested. "If ever we're to have luncheon——"

"Here is something against the wall!" Nancy interrupted excitedly.

She stooped to pick it up. Her exclamation of wonderment caused Bess and George to move closer. Nancy held up a slightly soiled photograph of a small boy wearing a white sailor suit.

"Girls, this is the same child whose picture was in Mrs. Alexandra's miniature!" she cried, her voice perplexed. "Do you suppose she is related to Francis Baum?"

"Haven't the slightest idea," replied Bess, shrugging her shoulders. "And look! There's a hamburger stand. George and I have an engagement at three o'clock, so we ought to eat."

"Please do," begged Nancy. "I want to go to Faber's first, and also turn in this picture to the police."

Her chums left to get a quick meal. Nancy went on alone and resumed her search for the antique shop. She came to it at last, an inconspicuous, but neat little place, on a quiet street. A bell jingled musically as she entered.

From a rear workroom emerged a little man with stooped shoulders. Smiling a welcome, he asked what he might do for the young lady. Nancy explained that she was looking for a gift for her father, and handed him the business card with Mrs. Alexandra's message on it.

"Oh, Madame sent you herself?" the shop owner beamed, speaking with a noticeable accent. "Ah, yes, I am honored to serve you. I may have something in my humble shop which will please your father."

The little man moved briskly about the cluttered room, shaking his head as he examined various objects.

"No, I have nothing suitable," he said at length. "You must give me a few days."

Before leaving the shop, Nancy decided to show the man the photograph she had found near the apartment house. She inquired if he knew whose picture it might be.

Old Mr. Faber stared at the child in the sailor suit, his hands trembling as he took the photograph.

"Where did you get this?" he asked tensely. "Tell me, please—tell me at once!"

CHAPTER II

THE JEWELER'S STORY

ASTONISHED by the tone of Mr. Faber's voice and his interest in the photograph, Nancy readily told how it had come into her possession.

"Unbelievable!" the antique dealer murmured. "You say this picture was stolen from a young man named Francis Baum?"

"I feel quite certain it fell from his wallet," Nancy replied, and waited eagerly for the man to reveal more.

"Can you describe this person?" the shop owner pleaded. "Did Francis Baum bear any resemblance to this delicate-faced lad of the photograph?"

"Why, not that I noticed. Mr. Baum is tall and has a dark complexion. There was nothing distinctive about him."

"Faces often change so much in expression as boys attain manhood that it would be hard to identify them," the shopkeeper murmured. "The age of Francis Baum?"

"Well, it's difficult to say. He might be in his late twenties—possibly in his early thirties."

Nancy's curiosity had grown steadily as Mr. Faber questioned her. She longed to ask a few of her own, but wisely waited. Within a few minutes the shop owner's excitement subsided somewhat, and he offered an explanation

"You wonder perhaps why I ask you so many questions," he said. "The answers concern the happiness of Mrs. Alexandra. You see, the lad of this photograph is her long-lost grandson!"

"Please tell me more about it," Nancy urged, her eyes sparkling in anticipation.

"Years ago, when revolution came to the dear lady's country, the little lad of the picture was taken away secretly by his faithful nurse. His mother and father, his sisters, the entire family—except the grandmother—perished at the hands of the enemy."

"How dreadful!" Nancy murmured.

"Those were terrifying years," the antique dealer resumed sadly. "Madame Alexandra, through the aid of loyal friends, escaped from the country. Since then she has devoted herself to a search for her missing grandson."

"The nurse has never been traced?"

"It is believed that she came to America, but here the trail ends. If Madame Alexandra's grandson still lives, he must be a young man. You understand now how important it is that we find Francis Baum?"

"Indeed I do," Nancy responded instantly. "I'll gladly help you trace him."

The offer was a more generous one than Mr.

Faber realized, for he seldom read the newspapers. Therefore he did not know of the girl's reputation as an amateur detective.

Nancy came naturally by her love of mystery, for she was the daughter of Carson Drew, a well-known lawyer, who often handled criminal cases. Her mother had died many years before, and ever since Nancy could remember, the household had been managed for her and her father by capable Hannah Gruen.

Hannah frequently remarked that her young charge "just couldn't be held down." At any rate, Nancy had solved many mysteries. Her first case was known to River Heights as "The Secret of the Old Clock," and her most recent adventure, "The Quest of the Missing Map."

"Will Francis Baum be difficult to find?" the elderly man questioned her anxiously.

"He shouldn't be," Nancy assured him. "No doubt his name and address are in the telephone directory."

Acting upon the suggestion, Mr. Faber called to an assistant in the back room. He requested that the book be brought to him at once. Ivan, a youth of twenty, with a pleasant grin, soon appeared, bearing the district directory. However, Baum's name was not listed in it.

"Never mind, I'll trace him somehow," Nancy consoled the antique dealer. "The policeman who recovered the stolen wallet must have his address."

"I know so little of how such matters are handled," the shopkeeper said rather help-

lessly. "If you find Francis Baum, I will reward you richly."

"Oh, I don't want a reward," Nancy protested with a laugh. "I'll find him just for the
fun of it, and to help Mrs. Alexandra."

Mr. Faber was not to be put aside so easily.

"I will repay you in some way, maybe by
obtaining a handsome gift for your father. A
'gentleman's box,' perhaps?"

"I am sure he would like it."

"When Mr. Faber says a 'gentleman's box'
he means something very special," contributed
Ivan, grinning at Nancy. "In Europe his
father and grandfather were famous jewelers
who made many pieces for royal families."

"Quiet, lad!" Mr. Faber reproved, although
not with displeasure.

"For a prince, Mr. Faber's father once made
a wonderful little train," Ivan went on undis-
turbed. "The locomotive was of platinum, and
the cars were gold. It ran, too."

"And was Mrs. Alexandra's Easter egg
made by your father, Mr. Faber?" Nancy
asked in awe.

"Ah, so you have seen it!" commented the
shop owner, smiling broadly.

"Only the outside. Not the contents."

"Madame Alexandra's Easter egg was indeed made by my famous father," Mr. Faber
declared. "It contains a most unusual object.
You must ask her to disclose the secret."

"I really don't know her well enough for
that," Nancy responded.

"If you find her lost grandson, no favor will be too great to ask," smiled the shop owner. "Ah, you surely must see the wonderful contents of her Easter egg. The gift was presented to her by her king son."

Nancy wondered if she had heard correctly.

"A king?" she repeated in bewilderment. "Then Mrs. Alexandra——"

Mr. Faber looked slightly dismayed. "Have I revealed information of which you had no knowledge?"

"I had no idea that Mrs. Alexandra was of royal blood."

"I assumed that you knew," the shopkeeper said quietly. "Madame Alexandra prefers that no special deference be shown her. She does not mind if a few discreet people know who she is, but if her true identity should become known to everyone, she would be subjected to attentions she wishes to avoid."

"I understand. I'll do everything I can to help her, too," Nancy promised without hesitation.

A few minutes later she left the shop, still excited by the amazing story Faber had told her. Forgetting that she had had no lunch, she went directly to the Central Police Station.

To her disappointment no record had been made of Francis Baum's address. Captain McGinnis promised that he would instruct the officer who had seen Baum to be on watch for the young man, and asked Nancy to keep the faded photograph.

Throughout the afternoon she searched diligently, inquiring at every hotel in River Heights. At length, sheer weariness forced her into a coffee shop not far from the river docks.

"Finding Francis Baum isn't going to be as easy as I thought," she reflected, nibbling a sandwich the waitress had brought. "In fact, Mrs. Alexandra may have to wait some time to see her grandson."

Through an open window Nancy absently watched a ferryboat tie up at the dock. Passengers alighted, and others boarded the vessel.

Suddenly the girl's gaze was drawn to a young man who looked familiar. For a moment Nancy could not remember where she had seen him before. Then in a flash she knew! He was the thief who had snatched Francis Baum's wallet!

Dropping a fifty-cent piece on the table to pay her check, Nancy hurriedly left the coffee shop. As she reached the street, she saw the man board the ferry.

"There he is!" she thought excitedly. "Or maybe he's that other fellow who was mistaken for the thief!"

Nancy could not be certain, and before she could decide what to do, a series of short blasts from the boat's whistle warned her that the ferry was about to leave. There was no time to think about the matter. The man would escape if she did not act instantly.

Breaking into a run, Nancy reached the dock

a moment before the gate was closed. Scarcely had she run to the crowded deck than the ropes were cast off, and the vessel edged away from shore.

Regaining her breath, the girl gazed about in search of the man she suspected was the thief. He was nowhere to be seen.

Thinking that he might have gone to the lunch counter, she looked there, but without success.

In despair she returned to the deck. During the past few minutes there had been a sudden change in the weather, and now Nancy was nearly blown from her feet by a strong gust of wind. The water had become rough, and the little ferryboat was churning through choppy waves.

"Looks as if we're in for a bad blow," remarked a passenger who leaned over the railing. "Hope we reach the opposite shore before it strikes us."

Nancy nodded as she scanned the clouds. She had worn no coat, and began to shiver in her thin, white linen dress. A few moments later she completely forgot her discomfort when she caught a glimpse of the suspect. He was walking away from her along the port railing. The girl quickened her step to overtake him.

Before Nancy could reach the man, a huge wave struck the ferryboat. Passengers were thrown off balance. Several women screamed. The next instant it grew dark. A blinding flash of lightning was followed by a deluge of rain, which blotted out all view of the river and other boats.

Gasping, Nancy tried to find shelter in the cabin, but others ahead of her jammed the passageway. The man she had tried to reach no longer could be seen in the milling throng.

Suddenly a ship's bell clanged. From off the port bow came the deep-throated toot of another whistle. The ferryboat swerved sharply to avoid a collision, but not in time.

There was a terrific impact as the two boats crashed into each other. Flung sideways, Nancy went rolling on the tilted deck.

CHAPTER III

A LOST FORMULA

STRUGGLING to her feet, Nancy grasped an iron railing for support. All about her women and children screamed in terror, and passengers trapped in the cabin fought to escape.

"Be calm, everyone!" shouted the captain through a megaphone, trying to avert a panic. "The ship won't sink. We'll reach the dock safely."

Nancy relayed his message to those about her. She assisted women to their feet, and comforted children who were crying in fright.

As it became evident that the vessel had not been damaged below the water line, the passengers became less panicky. But they jammed the decks while the crippled boat steamed slowly back toward River Heights.

In vain Nancy gazed about, searching for the suspected thief. He was nowhere in sight, and in despair the girl decided that she could not hope to locate him in the crowd. Then, just as the ferryboat grated against the dock, she saw the fellow not far ahead of her.

He stood close beside a man whose right leg had been injured. To her disgust, the suspect stealthily reached his hand into the other's coat pocket and removed a billfold.

"Stop, thief!" Nancy shouted, but so great was the commotion about her that the warning went unheard.

She tried to force her way forward, but the crowd kept her from moving more than a few feet. The boat now was ready to discharge passengers. To Nancy's chagrin the thief was one of the first to disembark.

By the time the Drew girl reached the dock, he had vanished. She was annoyed, but at least she could give the police a more accurate description of the pickpocket.

"He was of medium height, and had brown hair," she said to herself. "He walks with short, hurried steps."

It was still raining when Nancy left the dock. She ran toward a bus, but it was overcrowded, and the driver would take no more passengers. Finally she was able to hail a taxi, but by this time her clothing was soaked. Upon her arrival at home, Mrs. Gruen, the housekeeper, gasped at the girl's appearance.

"Nancy, what shall I do with you?" she said anxiously. "Will you never learn to carry an umbrella?"

"Never," the young detective laughed, kicking off a water-soaked shoe.

"Did you have a good luncheon?" the woman asked.

"A sandwich," Nancy replied, avoiding the housekeeper's gaze. "Please don't worry. It must be nearly dinnertime."

"It is," Mrs. Gruen nodded, "and if I am

not mistaken, there's your father now. I'm glad it has stopped raining."

A car had turned into the driveway. Nancy hurried to her room, wriggled into dry clothes, and ran down the stairs to greet her father.

"Why, Dad!" she exclaimed. "What's wrong? You look mad enough to eat some-one."

"I've lost my wallet," Mr. Drew said shortly. "I'm afraid it was stolen."

"Stolen! How did it happen?" Nancy asked, alert at once.

"I'm not absolutely certain. I didn't miss it until an hour ago."

"You didn't lose much money, I hope."

"Nearly three hundred dollars—not to men-tion several important papers."

"Three hundred dollars!" Nancy gasped, astonished that her father should be carrying such a large sum.

"The money wasn't mine," Mr. Drew ex-plained. "It was a donation to the needy River Heights Boys Club, to be used to buy equip-ment for the gymnasium. Now I'll have to pay the sum from my own pocket."

"That's a shame. Perhaps you dropped the wallet, and it will be returned," suggested Nancy.

"Not a chance," Mr. Drew concluded. "I'm sure it was stolen. In fact, as I think back, I recall that at noon, when I stood in line at a cafeteria, a man directly behind kept brushing against me."

"What did he look like, Dad?"

"Didn't notice in particular. A fellow of medium height with brown hair."

"Did he walk with short, quick steps?" Nancy asked eagerly.

"That seems to describe him," Mr. Drew agreed. "He got out of line and hurried off. Why all these questions? Do you know such a person?"

His daughter related her various experiences of the day. After she had told of the two thefts she had witnessed, Mr. Drew agreed that undoubtedly the pickpocket was the same man who had robbed him.

"Dad, I'll know that fellow if ever I see him again," Nancy concluded. "Would you like me to capture him for you?"

"Indeed I would," her father responded grimly. "I don't like putting up three hundred dollars. But let's forget this painful subject and get started for the picnic."

Nancy raised her eyebrows in surprise. "What picnic?" she inquired.

"Didn't I tell you? Some of my lawyer associates have arranged a father-daughter outing at Walden Park. We're due there pretty soon."

"I hope you didn't forget to tell Mrs. Gruen," Nancy laughed. "Picnics without food aren't much fun."

"Oh, I notified her by telephone," Mr. Drew smiled. "She'll have everything ready for us."

The lawyer's prediction was correct. Hastening to the kitchen, Nancy found the housekeeper tucking a thermos bottle into a well-filled hamper.

"At least you'll be spared a few dishes tonight," the girl laughed, picking up the heavy basket.

"I hope you won't find it wet at the park," the housekeeper called as the two left.

Fortunately the late afternoon sun was drying the ground quickly. Mr. Drew's good humor had returned as he walked with Nancy to the picnic grounds. Upon arriving, they found a group of eight well-known River Heights lawyers and their daughters already assembled.

The Drews were given an enthusiastic welcome but teased about being late. When they heard the story of the stolen wallet, the men became grave.

"It is no laughing matter," declared one of them, who was counsel for a private detective agency. "During the past two weeks River Heights has had an alarming increase in petty thievery. It's time something is done."

"You're right," agreed Mr. Drew. "Well, my Nancy says she's going to catch one of the pickpockets."

"And she probably will," said Ida Trevor, who admired the girl very much.

"At any rate, I'd like to get back the money for the Boys Club," Nancy declared.

Following the picnic supper, there were

games of competition for the fathers and their daughters. Victory crowned the efforts of the Drews in several of them.

However, in a short race they lost to Judge and Marian Howells. As they crossed the finish line a compact, which the judge was keeping for his daughter, fell from his pocket. The enamel cover broke in half.

"There, I've done it!" the man exclaimed. "Why can't these girls of ours have pockets large enough for their beauty gadgets?"

"What we need is an enamel which is non-crackable," said Mr. Drew.

"Many years ago such an enamel was developed," said the judge. "But, unfortunately, the process by which it was made is not known today. If the formula could be found, there would be countless uses for it."

Launching into the history of various enamel processes, he told of its early use by the Egyptians, Babylonians and Romans.

"There was a revival of the art in the nineteenth century, and beautiful, unbreakable pieces were made. But that method too has been lost."

"Do you suppose it ever will be recovered?" Nancy asked.

"Oh, it may turn up sometime," the judge laughed, "bringing its finder great riches."

Nancy was sorry when the picnic finally ended, for she had had a very good time. Yet the adventures of the day had given her much to think about, and she was glad to lie in bed and mull them over in her mind. She went to sleep wondering about the secret contained in the Easter egg.

At breakfast the next morning, while she was sipping some orange juice, the mailman arrived. Among the letters was one addressed to her. With mounting interest, she noted Mrs. Alexandra's name in the upper left-hand corner.

"Oh, I'm invited to tea!" she cried to Mrs. Gruen as she read the enclosed note. "Bess and George are to come with me! At four this afternoon!"

"That's nice," the housekeeper returned absently. "But I never knew that you enjoyed teas."

"This one will be exciting, I'm sure! Who knows? Mrs. Alexandra may show us the contents of her wonderful Easter egg!"

Carried away with enthusiasm, Nancy ran to telephone George and Bess. When she told them who the hostess for the tea was, they were amazed. There followed a lengthy discussion on their part of what to wear and how to act in the presence of royalty.

"I suggest that you conduct yourself as you would at any other tea," Mrs. Gruen advised, overhearing part of the conversation. "Tell them by all means to be natural."

Exactly at the hour of four, the invited guests presented themselves at Mrs. Alexandra's home. Anna opened the door, dropping a pretty curtsey as she bade them enter.

"Madame Marie awaits you in the drawing room," she said formally.

Bess and George felt less at ease than upon their first call, for they now knew that their hostess was of royal blood. Nevertheless, they soon overcame their shyness, for Mrs. Alexandra was most gracious.

"I am glad that you went to see Mr. Faber, Nancy," she smiled. "He told me on the telephone you had been there."

"He has many beautiful gifts in his shop," the girl replied. "I'm sure he'll find something appropriate for my father."

"Mr. Faber also told me that unwittingly he revealed my identity to you," the woman went on. "I beg of you not to mention it to anyone," she requested. "I came to your lovely town to avoid publicity."

"Is that why no one addresses you as Your Majesty, Mrs. Alexandra?" asked Bess. "It is customary, isn't it?"

"Yes, it is," the elderly lady responded, dropping her gaze to the floor for a moment. Then she raised her eyes and smiled. "When I came to your country, I decided to adopt its ways. So now I am Mrs. Alexandra. Only Anna cannot bring herself to this. We compromised," the woman added, lines of amusement showing around the corners of her mouth, "and she addresses me as Madame Marie."

With the arrival of tea, Nancy and her chums tried not to stare at the handsome silver service which the faithful servant placed before her

mistress with great ceremony. Never had they
seen such exquisite work. On one side of the
teapot was engraved a pheasant, while on the
other was a monogram, combined with a golden
royal crown.

To the further amazement of the girls, Anna
washed each tiny cup and saucer before handing the china to her mistress. Carefully she
dried the lovely pieces on a special towel of
linen, finished with dainty lace.

"An Old World custom," Mrs. Alexandra
explained, smiling. "The towel Anna uses was
handloomed by a dear friend. You see it has my
initials with the royal insignia above it."

As the girls sipped their tea and ate delicious, frosted cakes, their hostess spoke rather
sadly of present day life in her native land, so
changed from the past. Then, throwing aside
the mood of depression, she chatted animatedly
of her various art treasures. She seemed particularly fond of a rich gold and blue tapestry,
showing a gay ballet scene.

"This piece was woven especially for me
when I resided in the palace," she told the
girls. "I value it almost as highly as my precious Easter egg."

Nancy's gaze roved swiftly to the cabinet
where the exquisite little ornament stood on its
gold pedestal. The girl longed to learn its
secret, yet hesitated to make the request.

"Anna, please bring the Easter egg to me,"
Mrs. Alexandra requested, almost as if she had
read Nancy's thoughts.

The servant obeyed, placing the object on a mahogany table in front of her mistress.

"Now I shall show you a truly remarkable treasure," Mrs. Alexandra said softly. "Watch if you would know the secret contained within!"

CHAPTER IV

ROYAL TREASURES

As NANCY, Bess, and George waited expectantly, Mrs. Alexandra raised the lid of the
enamel Easter egg. Inside, rising from a nest
of velvet, was a tiny tree set with emeralds.
Upon a jeweled branch was perched a deli-
cately fashioned nightingale.

"How lovely!" Bess exclaimed, and the
other girls murmured in awe.

Mrs. Alexandra pressed a concealed spring
and the nightingale began to sing. The song
was brief and somewhat artificial, but nevertheless amazing.

"I treasure this not only for itself, but because it was given to me by my son only a short
time before his untimely death," said Mrs.
Alexandra. "It is my hope that some day I
shall find my grandson and pass it on to him."

The woman then told briefly how the lad had
been taken away secretly by his faithful nurse
who sought to save him from cruel enemies.

"Michael would be nearly thirty years old
now," she murmured. "Yet if I were to see
him tomorrow, I feel confident I would recognize him."

Nancy had not intended to tell the story of

Francis Baum, fearing that it might prove to be another disappointment to this ex-queen mother. A moment later, however, Mrs. Alexandra revealed that Michael's nurse had had a photograph of the lad, identical to the one of the miniature. Excited by this information, Nancy spoke of her strange meeting with the young man.

"Perhaps he is my long-lost grandson!" the elderly lady declared in an agitated voice. "Tell me, did he resemble the boy in the picture?"

Nancy was compelled to reply that she had noticed no similarity.

"We must find the young man at once!" Mrs. Alexandra urged. "Even if he is not Michael, he may know what has become of him."

Nancy promised that she would do everything possible to trace her missing relative. Observing that the exciting conversation was tiring Mrs. Alexandra, she and her chums soon left the house.

"I feel as if I had been dreaming," Bess remarked. "What did you think of the Easter egg, Nancy?"

"It is beautiful," the other responded. "But to tell you the truth, I was a bit disappointed. The nightingale didn't sing as it should."

"I noticed the same thing!" agreed George. "Its voice didn't even sound like a bird's."

"Mrs. Alexandra seemed unaware of any flaw," Nancy returned thoughtfully. "Oh, well, the work was perfect otherwise. Who are we to criticize royal treasure?'' she laughed. ''My job is to find Francis Baum.''

Upon reaching home Nancy wrote down the incomplete name and address which she had glimpsed on the card in the young man's wallet. Curiously she stared at the letters:

thson

ter St.

''If I can only fill these out, I may be able to contact someone who is acquainted with Mr. Baum,'' she reflected. ''Wonder if the city directory will help.''

For an hour she pored over the volume, eliminating name after name. At length she came to one which arrested her attention—J. J. Smithson, 25 Water Street.

''That might be worth investigating,'' the girl decided, copying the address.

The next afternoon, accompanied by her chums Bess and George, she pedaled on her bicycle to Water Street in the business section.

J. J. Smithson proved to be the owner of a small shop. He readily answered Nancy's questions. Francis Baum had worked for him a few days. He had not seen the young man since, but assumed that he still lived at a Mrs. Kent's boarding house in the next block.

Nancy obtained the address, and the girls pedaled on. Their spirits soared, for they believed that their search for the missing prince was nearing its end. The stout landlady, to whom they presently talked, repeated Francis Baum's name and shook her head.

"He was here," she said regretfully, "but he moved out day before yesterday."

"Didn't he leave a forwarding address?" Nancy asked in despair.

"No, he didn't. I'll tell you how you might trace him, though. He has his clothes washed at the Eagle Home Laundry."

"Isn't that across the river?" Nancy inquired.

"Yes, it is. It's a long distance from here."

The girls thanked Mrs. Kent for the information, and then discussed what they should do. Neither Bess nor George was willing to make the long trip by bicycle.

"Let's go by ferryboat tomorrow," the former suggested, and this plan was agreed upon.

The girls pedaled toward home. Nancy chose a route past the apartment building where the pickpocket had nearly been caught.

"You don't expect him to be here!" gasped Bess.

"It won't hurt to look," decided Nancy.

Windows on the lower floor were open wide. As the girls passed near them, they were startled to hear angry voices inside the dwelling.

"You can't hide here!" a man shouted.

"What can be wrong?" Nancy asked, pulling up beside the building.

"Sounds like an argument," responded George, likewise stopping her bicycle.

"You know the police may be watching this place!" one cried out. "You're not going to get me into trouble! Clear out!"

"What do you make of it, Nancy?" Bess whispered anxiously.

"It's my guess the pickpocket may be hiding in there," her chum replied. "Perhaps he has a pal who is afraid of being caught."

The argument waxed warmer, but the girls heard no more, for the window suddenly was slammed down. The action stimulated Nancy.

"George, you and Bess go for a policeman! Bring one here as quickly as you can."

"What will you do?" Bess inquired nervously.

"I'll stay here and keep watch. Better still, I'll go inside the apartment house and see what I can find out."

"Do be careful," George warned as she and Bess hurried away. "Those men may be desperate characters."

The instant the girls had gone, Nancy hid her bicycle in a clump of bushes. She then walked around the corner to the front of the building and entered. The outer lobby was deserted. Finding the inner door unlocked, she went inside.

"I wonder which apartment the men are in," she mused as she tiptoed down the dimly lighted hallway.

Nancy could hear no conversation, because several radios were playing loudly. She had no time to do any investigating, for at that moment a door a little distance away from her opened. A man rushed out, slamming it behind him.

He resembled the pickpocket!

Nancy wanted to get a better look at him, before he might see her, so she gazed about for a place in which to hide. Near her was a telephone booth. She darted inside.

"If he *is* the pickpocket, I'll follow him out of the building!" she decided.

Unfortunately the man spied her, and must have become suspicious of her intentions. With an angry gleam in his eye, he ran forward.

"He *is* the pickpocket," Nancy concluded. "He saw me from the window, and knows I heard what was said!"

Fearful that he meant harm, she slammed shut the glass-paneled door of the booth. To her consternation the man took a piece of wood from his pocket, wedging it under the crack.

"There! How do you like that?" he sneered.

Nancy pushed with all her strength against the door, but it would not move. The wedge held fast. She was trapped!

"Guess that will teach you not to pry into what doesn't concern you!" the pickpocket taunted her.

With a satisfied laugh, he ran from the building.

CHAPTER V

THE MYSTERIOUS JEWEL BOX

ANNOYED as she was by the man's actions in keeping her from following him, Nancy did not believe herself to be a prisoner in the booth. She thought she could drop a nickel into the telephone box and summon help. But a search of her purse dismayed the girl. She did not have a single coin with her.

Thoroughly alarmed, Nancy pounded on the door. Her cries went unheard, for the radios playing in the various apartments completely drowned her voice.

"Oh, dear, that pickpocket will be blocks away before I get out of here!" she thought in despair.

The wedge beneath the door could not be moved, even when she pried at it with a nail file. The bit of steel broke in her hand.

As the tiny booth became hot and stuffy, Nancy's irritation changed to desperation. Somehow she had to get out.

"I'll smash the glass with the heel of my shoe!" she decided.

Fortunately at that very moment Bess and George arrived at the apartment house with a policeman. Nancy's shouts drew their attention to her plight.

"The thief escaped!" she gasped as the officer jerked open the door. "He locked me in here, and then ran out the front way."

"Front way? Why, when we were way up the street, we saw a man climb through one of the windows," George said in astonishment. "We thought he was the pickpocket. Officer Kelly chased him, but he had too long a start."

"That must have been the pickpocket's companion in the apartment," Nancy responded in a discouraged tone.

"Which door did the fellow you saw come out of?" asked the policeman.

"One of those back there," Nancy pointed. "I think the third."

Officer Kelly rapped sharply on it. For several seconds there was no answer, and he was about to try again when the door opened a tiny crack. A woman in a dressing gown peered into the hall.

"What do you want?" she asked in a frightened voice.

The policeman walked into the untidy living room.

"There's no one here except me," the woman whined. "Who are you after?"

"A pickpocket who hid in this building," Kelly answered briefly.

"Not in my rooms," the woman maintained "You musta got your wires crossed."

"Didn't someone jump from a window here?"

"No!"

"Do you live alone?" the officer inquired.

"Well, no, I got a husband," the woman answered. "He has a ne'er-do-well cousin who sticks around here sometimes when he's in trouble."

"Trouble?"

"Cordova has a way of gettin' mixed up in things," the woman answered with a shrug. "But I ain't sayin' it's dishonest, and it's none of my affair. He ain't here now, and I wish you'd leave me alone!"

Officer Kelly asked a few additional questions before leaving, but he could not get an admission from her that either the husband or the cousin had been there a few moments ago. Neither he nor the three girls accepted the woman's story as entirely true.

"I'll check up on her," the policeman promised as he bade Nancy and her chums good-by, "and question some of the other people here. We'll keep watch of this building and try to catch that pickpocket."

Bess and George, who had an errand at the Public Library, decided to go on alone. Left to herself, Nancy pedaled slowly toward home. She decided to stop at Mr. Faber's shop, and was nearly there when she met her father.

"Fancy meeting you here!" she laughed, halting.

"I've been interviewing a client in this district," Mr. Drew replied.

"Shall I give you a ride home on the handlebars?"

"No, thank you," he declined with a laugh. "But I'll go home with you. I'm through for the day."

"Then I have an idea!" Nancy cried, her gaze roving to a creaking business sign which bore Faber's name. "You must come into this shop. It is the most interesting place." To herself she was saying, "Maybe I can find out what he'd like for a birthday present."

"I'm not going to buy anything!" insisted the lawyer.

"I'll attend to that part," laughed Nancy.

Giving Mr. Drew no opportunity to protest, his daughter steered him into the establishment. Mr. Faber seemed genuinely pleased to meet the lawyer, and at a wink from the girl immediately questioned him as to his likes and dislikes in art objects.

"Oh, anything goes with me," Mr. Drew replied pleasantly. "But I'd like to look around. My daughter admires your shop very much."

"I'm glad to know that," the little man beamed. As Mr. Drew moved off to view the collection in the overcrowded shop, Mr. Faber whispered to the girl, "A 'gentleman's box' would be exactly right for your distinguished-looking father."

Nancy, pleased at the compliment, asked what a "gentleman's box" was.

"In ancient times a gentleman was known by the personal chest he carried," the old dealer resumed, warming to his subject, "a lady by her jewel box. Jewels always have been a convenient kind of wealth to carry—far easier than money. Rulers forced to flee from their countries in time of war have saved part of their fortunes that way."

"And sold them to get money?" Nancy asked.

"Exactly. Also, in olden days, wars were won and lost because of rare gems—for instance, the Kohinoor diamond."

"That enormous diamond has an interesting story," said Mr. Drew, overhearing the remark.

"Ah, yes, a fantastic tale but true," agreed Mr. Faber. "It's history began some six or seven hundred years ago, when the stone was found in a river of South India. Since then it has changed hands many times, but usually only through the envy and greed of war."

"How did the diamond receive its name?" Nancy asked.

"That, too, is connected with war. A Persian conqueror captured a ruler named Mohammed, who owned the gem at the time. What he really came for was the stone, but he could not find it. Finally a woman told him that the gem was hidden in the folds of the turban worn by Mohammed night and day."

"I suppose the Persian then took it by force?" Nancy remarked.

"No," Mr. Faber corrected her. "He tried another method. I believe he had more pleasure doing it that way. He pretended to be Mohammed's friend, even promising to restore his throne to him. Then he slyly suggested that, as a token of esteem, they exchange turbans. Mohammed dared not refuse. When the other found the diamond, he cried 'Kohinoor!' which means Mountain of Light.''

"And carried the gem home with him!" added Mr. Drew.

"Then what became of the diamond?" asked Nancy.

"Oh, it is a long, long story," replied the antique dealer. "You come again some day, and I will tell you more. Once it was hidden under the plaster of a prison cell and found by a guard who scratched himself on it."

"And wasn't some queen put into a dungeon and starved until her husband sold the diamond to obtain her release?" asked Mr. Drew.

"That is true," replied Mr. Faber.

"Where is the Kohinoor now?" questioned Nancy.

"At present it reposes peacefully in the jewel room of the Tower of London."

"Speaking of jewels, Mr. Faber," said Nancy, "how was Mrs. Alexandra able to bring so many valuables with her when she fled from her country?"

"Madame is a very clever woman," the antique shop owner replied. "She carried a small fortune secreted in a jewel box. It was so unique that it deceived everyone. Her only other possession was the handsome Easter egg case."

"But I saw so many lovely things in her

home," Nancy declared. "Brocades, tapestries, tables, bric-a-brac."

"All of those treasures were recovered after Mrs. Alexandra reached America. For years I was busy locating her family possessions which turned up in odd corners of the world. She wanted them so badly that she sold many of her jewels to obtain them."

"How was she able to leave Europe?" Nancy inquired thoughtfully. "Did she wear a disguise when she crossed the border from her country?"

"She dressed as a peasant woman," Mr. Faber explained. "That was why the soldiers were not suspicious when they examined the Easter egg and the jewel box. They assumed that both objects were cheap novelties."

"You say Mrs. Alexandra was able to save a, fortune?" inquired Mr. Drew, his curiosity aroused.

"A small one. She had many jewels, and by selling them one at a time, she has been able to live comfortably."

"I hope some day Mrs. Alexandra will show me her jewel case," Nancy said wistfully. "I did see the contents of the Easter egg. The singing nightingale was unique."

"The *singing* nightingale?" Mr. Faber echoed. "But the little bird does not sing."

"Oh, but it does! My chums heard the song as well as I. However, we all thought it did not sound just right."

"That is very strange, very strange," murmured the shop owner. "When my father made the enameled egg years ago the nightingale did not sing. I shall ask Mrs. Alexandra about it when next I see her."

Nancy was so deeply interested in the matter that during the evening she called upon the woman. After reporting a little progress in searching for Francis Baum, the girl tactfully brought up the subject of the singing nightingale.

"Oh, I think the little bird always has sung," the woman answered after Mr. Faber's conversation had been repeated to her. "I must admit that for many years I did not realize this. Then one day I accidentally touched the spring that controls the mechanism."

"Mr. Faber thinks that his father did not intend the bird to sing."

"I fear that he is mistaken."

"Then there's no mystery connected with it?" Nancy's voice disclosed disappointment.

"Not to my knowledge," Mrs. Alexandra replied. The laughter faded suddenly from her eyes. "In my life there is only one mystery," she said sadly. "The mystery of what became of my beloved grandson. Find him for me and my gratitude will be boundless."

CHAPTER VI

TRACING THE HEIR

MRS. ALEXANDRA's plea stirred Nancy to greater effort to find the missing Francis Baum. She set off early the next morning with George and Bess to the town across the river where the Eagle Laundry was located. There she obtained the young man's new address.

"I hope he'll be there," said George excitedly, starting off.

As the girls searched for the boarding house, Nancy gaily hummed a song. It was faintly recognizable as the tune sung by Mrs. Alexandra's nightingale.

"I wish you would forget that thing," George complained at last.

"Wish I could," Nancy responded cheerfully. "The tune has been running through my head ever since I first heard it."

"Try whistling *Home Sweet Home* for a change," laughed Bess.

The girls had arrived at 35 Cornell Avenue, a boarding house with a wide veranda covered by vines. In response to their knock, a stout woman, whose hands were red and puffy from work, came to the door.

"You want to rent rooms?" she asked before they could speak.

"No, we are trying to trace a young man by the name of Francis Baum," Nancy explained. "I understand he lives here."

"Yes, he rents a room upstairs," the landlady agreed, and then plunged the girl's hopes downward by adding, "He's not here now, though. He had to go away for a few days on business."

Nancy was disappointed. How long would it be before she could interview him?

"I believe I'll leave a message," she said thoughtfully. "Tell Mr. Baum when he returns that I have a picture for him—one which I think he lost from his wallet. My name is Nancy Drew."

"I'll tell him," the landlady promised.

"Please ask him to telephone me at once in River Heights or come for the photograph," Nancy went on, giving her address.

"I'll tell him, but whether or not he'll do it I couldn't say. He hasn't phoned a girl once since he came here, " she smirked. "He's kind of queer, anyhow."

Behind Nancy's back, Bess and George giggled. It amused them that the landlady had assumed their chum to be romantically interested in Francis Baum.

"You say he is rather queer?" Nancy pursued the matter. "In what way?"

"Oh, he keeps so much to himself," the woman answered. "It seems funny to me that he always locks his suitcase and hides the keys. I said to my husband, 'You can bet that man has something to hide.' So far I can't find out what it is."

"Does Mr. Baum have many callers?"

"A friend once in awhile—never any girl friends," the landlady replied.

"Just give him my message, please," Nancy returned rather curtly.

Blushing, she turned away, walking ahead of Bess and George, who grinned broadly.

"Now, no wisecracks!" she tried to forestall her chums.

"Why, Nancy," George said in mock reproach. "We didn't know you were trying to track down a husband of royal blood! So you crave a title?"

"And after your marriage we'll have to bow and say, 'Your Majesty,' " teased Bess. "No wonder you pursue poor Francis Baum so relentlessly."

"Have your fun," Nancy said cheerfully. "My hour will come!"

The girls took a ferryboat to their side of the river, then separated. Nancy, approaching her home a few minutes later, observed that Mrs. Gruen was entertaining two callers on the veranda. At first the girl thought she had never seen either of the young ladies before. But as she reached the house, she gave a joyous shout.

"Helen Corning!" she greeted her old friend and former classmate. "If you aren't a treat for the natives! When did you get back?"

"Only yesterday," Helen answered, giving Nancy an affectionate hug and kiss. "And what an exciting trip Dad and I had coming

home from Europe! His work took so long
that we stayed on and on. I spent most of my
time studying in Paris.''

''I should say you devoted yourself to the
dress shops! My, that's a stunning suit you're
wearing!''

''Katherine Kovna designed and made it for
me,'' Helen said proudly. ''Nancy, I want you
to know Katherine. We met in Europe, and I
talked her into coming to this country and stay-
ing with me for awhile.''

Nancy smilingly greeted the pretty girl, who
bowed in a shy way and spoke a few stilted
words.

''Katherine has a heart of gold and she's
wonderfully talented,'' Helen said, fearing that
her friend was not creating a favorable impression. ''As soon as she masters English a trifle
better, she's destined to make a name for herself!''

''First I must find work,'' Katherine declared soberly.

''Katherine is an orphan,'' Helen explained.
''Her parents were killed when the government
of their country was overturned. She expects
to earn a living as a dress designer.''

''I do so hope,'' murmured the foreign girl.
''But it seem hard——''

''All you lack is self-confidence,'' Helen interrupted severely. ''Why, you have more
talent than any dressmaker in River Heights!
Once you get a start, money will pour into your
lap.''

The start, Nancy soon learned, had been

carefully planned by her friend. Helen intended to entertain at a series of luncheons in honor of Katherine.

"Each time I shall wear a marvelous gown designed especially for me," Helen went on enthusiastically. "Everyone will ask where I bought it, and I'll tell them of Katherine's work. Then the orders will roll in!"

"You Americans," smiled the European girl, "you are so fast. You sweep off the feet!"

The others laughed.

"If I am invited to one of the parties, I'll need a new dress," said Nancy, a twinkle in her eye.

"You know you're invited! And Katherine can measure you now," Helen said at once. "As her business manager, I accept the order. The price—well, we'll give you a special discount, Nancy."

The Drew girl ran to get a tape measure from the sewing basket. Katherine made the various notations on a slip of paper, and sketched a few ideas for consideration. As she tried to decide which one she liked best, Nancy casually hummed a few bars of the nightingale's song. The young designer listened attentively.

"That melody!" she murmured. "What is its name?"

"So far as I know, it has none," Nancy answered. "I'll try to sing the words, but I don't know what they mean."

She sang a few of the syllables as she remembered them.

"That sound almost like words in my native language," Katherine announced. "But they make no meaning to me."

Nancy gazed at the girl with startled eyes. Until that moment it had not occurred to her that the mechanical nightingale might be trying to say something.

"Katherine, you've just given me a wonderful idea!" she exclaimed. "I can't explain it now, but I think I may need your help."

"I gladly do anything."

"You're a dear," Nancy said, squeezing the other's hand. "There is someone I very much want you to meet—a Mrs. Alexandra. I shall ask her if I may take you to see her tomorrow."

Katherine replied that she would be very happy to go, providing the call did not interfere with the dressmaking plans.

"We'll postpone the new gown if necessary," Nancy answered gaily. "This is really important, Katherine. You may be able to help me solve a mystery!"

"Nancy never allows anything to crowd a mystery from her calendar," laughed Helen. "You may as well resign yourself, Katherine."

After the two girls left, Nancy lost no time in telephoning to Mrs. Alexandra. As she had hoped, the lady graciously assured her that she might bring her friends to tea any afternoon she chose, but asked that her identity not be revealed.

"Then I should like to come tomorrow," the girl replied, and a moment later put down the instrument.

"If you can descend to earth for a moment, I wish you would go to the soda shop for some ice cream," Mrs. Gruen said as Nancy sat staring into space. "Queens and lost princes are all very romantic, but common folk have to eat!"

"A loaf of bread, did you say?" the girl inquired absently.

"A quart of ice cream," the housekeeper sighed. "And do try to get back before it melts."

"I'll prove to you that my slippers have little wings!" Nancy laughed, skipping away.

But she did not return as soon as she had expected she would. There were many people in the store, and it was several minutes before she was waited on.

"I guess Dad will be home by the time I get back," Nancy said to herself as she hurried along the street.

Sure enough, his car stood in the driveway. As she went toward the kitchen door, she noticed her father in his study. She was just about to call "hello" through the open window when she saw a sight which made her heart skip a beat.

A man seated in a chair opposite Mr. Drew was pointing a revolver at him!

CHAPTER VII

The Pickpocket's "Double"

"You'll be sorry if you don't pay my price!" the man was saying to Mr. Drew.

Nancy did not wait a second. Dropping the package of ice cream, she seized a rock from the flower garden beneath the window, and threw it directly at the gun. The weapon went spinning from the fellow's hand.

The girl scrambled through the window. Before the stranger could recover from his surprise, she snatched up the weapon and handed it to her father.

"Why, Nancy!" said Mr. Drew. "You—I——"

"This man is the pickpocket who stole Francis Baum's wallet!" she told her father. "I'll call the police."

"Oh, no you don't," said the accused person. "That revolver isn't loaded, and I meant no harm."

Nancy felt certain that the man was not telling the truth. She still was unconvinced that he had no motive, even when her father opened the weapon and she saw that it contained no bullets.

"I guess my life wasn't in danger," said Mr.

51

Drew, trying to relieve the situation, "but I do appreciate your trying to save me, Nancy dear."

"It's all a mistake," the caller insisted. "The truth is, I came here to see you, Miss Drew."

"To see me?" Nancy echoed, thoroughly bewildered. "But I did see you pointing the revolver directly at my father!"

"Not intentionally, Miss Drew. I was merely trying to sell it to him."

"That's true," said Mr. Drew. "He noticed my collection of antique firearms on the wall, and thought I might like to add this one to it."

"He's wanted by the police," Nancy insisted stubbornly. "Or is it possible," she turned to the caller, "that you're the man who looks so much like the pickpocket?" The man had crossed the room and she noted that he walked with a long stride and not short, hurried steps.

"Now you're beginning to see the light," the fellow smiled. "My name is Dorrance—David Dorrance. You saved me from arrest. As soon as I found out who you are, I came here to thank you."

"Nancy, I think you owe Mr. Dorrance an apology," Mr. Drew said. "I'm afraid this time you've made a mistake in your sleuthing."

"I truly am sorry," the girl replied, much embarrassed.

"Oh, I can't blame you for acting as you did," the caller responded, accepting the revolver which Mr. Drew handed him. "Several times I've been mistaken for that other fellow."

"He resembles you closely enough to be your twin," Nancy remarked. She stared hard at the young man, trying to memorize his features to avoid future misunderstanding.

"It's hard on me having the police and young lady detectives always after me," Dorrance resumed. "Why, those energetic chums of yours chased me a block, no doubt mistaking me for the pickpocket."

"My friends pursued you?" Nancy again became alert. "Was that when you left an apartment house on Water Street yesterday?"

"Oh, no, I haven't been near there, except the day Mr. Baum's wallet was stolen. The chase was about an hour ago."

"Why did you run?" asked Nancy pointedly.

"I didn't. It was only after I'd boarded a bus that I realized they were after me," the man laughed.

Nancy decided that she had been unduly suspicious of him, especially after he explained that he bought and sold antique weapons as a hobby. The revolver she had knocked from his hand had been purchased at a shop only a short time before. Nancy recalled having seen a similar one at Faber's establishment.

"I don't see how I made such a mistake," she said in apology. "I'm afraid it may happen again, too, for you certainly resemble that pickpocket very closely."

"Why not arrange a set of signals?" Dorrance joked.

"Not a bad idea," said Mr. Drew.

"If I ever mistake you again for the thief, wave a handkerchief," directed Nancy. "Then I'll know who you are."

"I'll do it," the young man agreed. "Well, I'll be off now. Good-by."

A moment later he left the house. Nancy went at once to rescue the half-melted ice cream she had dropped outside. She carried it to the icebox, then returned to the study.

"What do you think of David Dorrance?" she asked her father.

"I wasn't much impressed with him as a personality," the lawyer replied. "However, I must say he took your accusation in a rather sporting way."

Nancy perched herself on an arm of her father's chair. "I dislike him myself," she said feelingly. "I'll always have a picture of him pointing a gun at you! He scared me horribly."

"I feel as grateful as I would if you actually had saved my life, Nancy," Mr. Drew added kindly. "Well, here's Hannah, so dinner is ready. Let's forget this unpleasant episode," he added, tucking one of Nancy's arms under his own and walking into the dining room with her.

The following afternoon Nancy took Helen Corning and her house guest, Katherine, to call on Mrs. Alexandra. To Nancy's delight the girls made a favorable impression. More than that, Katherine soon realized who the woman was, and an animated conversation between the two began at once in a foreign tongue.

"Mrs. Alexandra and I—we are from the same country," Katherine announced to the girls. "I been away from it long time. You must excuse—we have much to say."

The other two did not mind being excluded. They were pleased because Katherine was so happy. Nancy pointed out the various art objects in the room to Helen, who was fascinated with their beauty.

Just before the girls were ready to leave, Anna took down the gold-encrusted Easter egg and pressed the tiny spring. The nightingale sang its strange little song.

Katherine listened attentively, but offered no comment other than polite admiration. The moment the three girls were on the street, Nancy eagerly asked her if the bird had sung any words.

"He use words of my native tongue, but they are not clear," the foreign girl answered with a troubled frown. "They have no—what you say, sense."

"Didn't you get any meaning out of them?" Nancy asked in disappointment.

Katherine paused a moment, then she smiled delightfully. "It sound silly, maybe, but the little bird seem to say, 'Clue in Jewel Box!'"

CHAPTER VIII

KATHERINE'S CLUE

"YES, the nightingale say, 'Clue in Jewel Box,' I believe," Katherine Kovna repeated in her halting English. "But that mean nothing."

"It may mean something very important!" Nancy corrected her excitedly.

"Of course the people of my native land—they have many secrets," smiled the foreign girl.

The remark brought back to Nancy's mind what Mr. Faber had told her about the elderly lady's escape from revolutionists with only the enameled Easter egg and a jewel box.

"There may be a connection between the two!" she thought. "The question is, does Mrs. Alexandra know that or not? She certainly didn't act as if she knew that the bird's song had any meaning."

The Drew girl decided that perhaps the "clue" was a political secret the woman could not reveal.

"Mrs. Alexandra and her possessions grow more mysterious each day," Nancy concluded to herself. "But maybe when Francis Baum turns up, many secrets will be revealed."

She had lapsed into silence as she considered the various unexplained bits of the strange trail she was following. A pickpocket with a double had led her to a lost prince. That man's grandmother held the secret to something which was being guarded carefully, judging from the trouble someone had taken to make the nightingale speak.

The girl was growing impatient to hear from Francis Baum. She wondered if the boarding house woman had failed to deliver the message which had been left for him.

"Nancy," said Helen, breaking in upon her friend's thoughts, "how would you like to wear a new gown at a fashion show?"

"As a model, you mean?" Nancy asked, rather surprised.

"Yes, Katherine has agreed to help with a three-day fashion exhibit at the Woman's Club. A special prize is to be awarded to the person who designs the most original and attractive dress."

"Of course I'll do it," promised Nancy readily. "When is the show?"

"It starts next Thursday. There will be three afternoon performances and another showing on Saturday night."

"Can you design and make a dress so soon, Katherine?" Nancy asked.

"I can try," the other replied. "I plan the right type for you."

"The fashion show will be a grand way in which to make Katherine's talents known," went on Helen. "Between you girls, you ought to win first prize."

"I am thinking of a design now—a modern one, but it have the touch of the Renaissance period," Katherine said dreamily. "An evening dress with a short train." She paused a moment. "Every detail I want correct, before I cut the beautiful material. I bring several yards with me from Europe."

The following afternoon Nancy went to the Corning home for the first fitting. Although the dress barely was started, she could tell that it would be beautiful.

"It's perfect," Helen praised in delight. "The lines are so simple and yet so smart."

"The blue of the flowered silk exactly match your eyes," Katherine said from a position on her knees. "I take a tuck here, and I shorten the train. Then tomorrow the gown is finished."

"And your reputation will be made!" Helen cried gaily. "With Nancy modeling the dress, you're certain to get many clients."

"I'll do my best to see that they flock your way," laughed Nancy. "I hope I shan't do something wrong, like tripping, as I parade before the judges!"

She knew that Katherine's success meant everything to her. For that reason, if for no other, she would do her best for the girl.

In the meantime, Nancy intended to devote every spare moment to the task of finding Francis Baum. As she sat with her father at the breakfast table the next morning, she de-

cided that she again would get in touch with the
landlady at his boarding house.

"Why so sober, Nancy?" Mr. Drew inquired,
pouring himself a second cup of coffee.

His daughter had no chance to reply. From
the front porch came a shrill scream, unmis-
takably the voice of Hannah Gruen.

"Now what?" demanded Mr. Drew, pushing
back his chair.

Thoroughly alarmed, he and Nancy ran to
the front door. A ferocious-looking police dog
was jumping around on the porch, and would
not let the housekeeper approach either the
steps or the door. Whenever she moved, the
animal leaped at her.

"Don't come outside!" the woman warned
Nancy and her father. "The dog may attack
you."

At this moment the animal turned of his own
accord and went down the steps. At once Hannah Gruen gained the safety of the hall.

"I was looking for the mail," she explained,
"when he came up behind me and growled.
I'm sorry I screamed, but the animal frightened me."

"I wonder where the dog came from?" said
Nancy.

The question was answered by the arrival of
a young man, who obviously was his master.

"Hope Rudy didn't frighten you," he apologized. "He broke away from me."

The voice struck Nancy as oddly familiar

Then her heart began to beat a little faster.
She recognized him as Francis Baum.

"Oh, good morning!" she cried, running
down the steps to greet him. "Aren't you Mr.
Baum?"

"I am," he admitted promptly. "And you
are Miss Drew, the girl who left a message
for me?"

"Yes, I've been hoping you would call."
With difficulty Nancy controlled her excitement,
forcing herself to speak in a calm, casual voice.
"I have a picture which I think belongs to
you."

"Of a boy in a sailor suit?"

"Yes, apparently it fell from your wallet
when it was stolen."

"I'm certainly glad you found it. It's important," Baum replied.

"Important?" asked Nancy, trying not to
show how eager she was to hear his answer.

"It may get me some relatives and a fortune
some day," the man boasted.

"We'd better go inside," said Mr. Drew.
"Have you had breakfast?" he inquired.

Nancy had told her father of her belief that
Francis Baum was the long missing heir.

"I could eat a bite or two," the caller accepted quickly.

Mrs. Gruen set an extra place at the table,
all the while eying Rudy with suspicion and
dislike. Mr. Baum had allowed the dog to follow him into the house.

Mr. Drew reopened the conversation by asking where their guest was born. Nancy was not surprised to hear that it was in Mrs. Alexandra's native land.

"When did you come to this country, Mr. Baum?" inquired her father.

"Don't remember exactly," the young man answered. "I was just a kid when my foster mother brought me to America. She always said I was the son of a king!"

"Is your foster mother living?" Nancy asked.

She tried not to notice that Mr. Baum was cramming buttered toast into his mouth and clattering the silverware noisily as he ate. Surely the nurse of a prince would have taught him better table manners.

"No, she died a good many years ago. I wouldn't mind locating some of my real folks, but I don't know how to do it."

This was Nancy's cue to say that she might be able to help him. The words did not come easily. She was rather dismayed to hear herself say in a tone not very friendly:

"Mr. Baum, if you have proper credentials— if you actually can prove you are the person in the photograph—I can lead you to your grandmother."

"Honestly? Where is she?" he demanded instantly.

"I can't tell you that until you offer some proof of your identity."

"I don't get it," Francis Baum said a trifle sullenly. "If you think I'm a fake, you've got me all wrong. I can prove who I am."

"Oh, I didn't mean to suggest that I doubt you," Nancy corrected hurriedly. "I have no reason for doing so."

"Bring your credentials to us just as soon as you can, Mr. Baum," said Carson Drew, his tone ending the interview. "And thank you for calling."

Hannah waited only until the young man and his dog were beyond hearing, before voicing a few remarks.

"If that man is a lost prince, then I am a queen! Did you see the way he gobbled his food? A few bites, indeed! He ate enough for six men!"

"You shouldn't begrudge him a little food," Mr. Drew reproved. "I judge he's poor, and probably hasn't eaten much recently."

"It was the way he ate that I didn't like," Mrs. Gruen continued. "And he didn't show any refinement at all."

"Obviously, Baum hasn't had the training we'd expect a prince to have," agreed Mr. Drew. "But no doubt he has had to shift for himself a long time."

"He talked rather well at first," Nancy remarked thoughtfully. "But toward the end he almost seemed like a different character."

"You forgot to give him the lost photograph," Mr. Drew reminded her.

"I didn't forget, Dad. I decided to keep it until I am sure of his claims."

"Then you distrust Baum?"

"Not exactly, Dad. I'll admit I don't like him. He bears not the slightest resemblance to the boy in the photograph."

"If you ask me, he's a fraud!" Hannah announced flatly. "Mark my words, he'll never show up with any credentials."

The housekeeper's prediction proved incorrect. Just at lunchtime Francis Baum returned, bearing a package which contained a letter written by his former nurse, and a small toy lamb with a jeweled collar. Much as she disliked to do so, Nancy felt compelled to invite the young man to stay for the noonday meal.

"When can I see my grandmother?" Francis Baum asked the girl as he ate ravenously.

"Very soon, I hope," she replied. "I will talk with her today, and show her the things you've brought."

"Why can't I see her myself?" he asked sullenly. "What's the idea of being so mysterious?"

"I have my reasons," Nancy returned. "If you expect me to help you, you'll have to wait."

"Acting sort of high and mighty, aren't you?" Baum said impatiently. "Don't you think I'm honest?"

"Your credentials seem satisfactory, Mr. Baum. Of course, only your grandmother can determine whether or not they are genuine."

"She'll recognize these things all right," he replied confidently.

Three o'clock found Nancy seated in Mrs. Alexandra's home with the letter spread out on a table between them. A lump came into her throat as she watched the old lady caress the toy lamb.

"My darling grandson played with this in his royal nursery," the sweet lady said, smiling through her tears. "I gave it to him myself on his third birthday."

"And the letter? Can you identify it, too?"

Mrs. Alexandra adjusted her eyeglasses and scanned the worn sheet of paper.

"Yes, this is the handwriting of my grandson's faithful nurse, Nada. There can be no question of it! The young man is my lost Michael! Have him pack his belongings at once, and come here to live."

"Oh, Madame Marie!" protested Anna faintly.

Nancy glanced quickly toward the servant. Mrs. Alexandra's decision apparently had dismayed her.

"I was only thinking that it might excite you to have your grandson in the house," Anna murmured in explanation. "Also, we have no room prepared for Prince Michael."

"That is true," agreed Mrs. Alexandra reluctantly. "When my grandson comes, we must show him every consideration. We will have a dinner in his honor," she added dreamily.

"Would it not be better to wait a day or two at least?" pleaded Anna.

"Very well," Mrs. Alexandra consented unwillingly. "But prepare for my grandson's arrival as quickly as you can. I shall write him a long letter of welcome."

Nancy ventured to suggest that it might be advisable to remove from the rooms some of the most valued antiques. Anna nodded approvingly, but Mrs. Alexandra seemed slightly displeased by the proposal.

"I am sure my grandson is to be trusted," she said coldly.

"Your grandson—yes," Nancy replied. "As for this Francis Baum, you are not certain yet that he is the missing prince. While his credentials seem perfect, it is barely possible he could have deceived us."

"I shall reflect upon your suggestion," Mrs. Alexandra said, her good humor restored.

Nancy held scant hope that the woman would order a removal of the treasures. She tried to bring up the subject of the singing nightingale and its strange message, but Mrs. Alexandra showed no willingness to discuss the matter. All her thoughts centered upon her grandson and plans for his homecoming.

"I will do what I can with Madame," Anna whispered to Nancy as the girl left the house. "But she is very determined once she makes up her mind. You are so right about the treasures. They should be hidden until we have more proof that this man is the true prince."

The afternoon was unusually sultry. Nancy walked slowly down the elm-shaded street. Reaching the business section, she paused at a small shop to drink a glass of cold lemonade. Suddenly from the next corner came the excited cries of a woman.

"My pocketbook!" she wailed. "That man snatched it! Stop him, someone!"

Pedestrians turned to see a young man in a brown suit running down the street, but no one acted quickly enough to stop him. Nancy saw the thief enter a department store.

"That man looks like the one who stole Francis Baum's wallet and probably Dad's!" she thought. "This is my chance to catch him!"

CHAPTER IX

Mistaken Identity

Confident that she could bring about the arrest of the pickpocket, Nancy followed him into the department store. Although the young man mingled with the crowd, she was able to spot him and keep him in sight. Then to her surprise, he paused at the necktie counter. He turned and looked at the girl.

"Good afternoon, Miss Drew," he murmured. Removing a white handkerchief from his vest pocket, he waved it and smiled.

Nancy was so chagrined that she went on without a word other than a perfunctory greeting. Again she had mistaken David Dorrance for the pickpocket! Not only was this embarrassing, but it made her doubt that she ever could make a positive identification of the thief.

"It's fortunate we arranged that handkerchief signal," she thought as she left the store. "Otherwise I would have caused the arrest of an innocent man."

For the next twenty minutes Nancy remained at the front entrance of the store, watching for the real pickpocket. She saw no one who remotely resembled him, and at length decided he had escaped by the side door. The chiming of a clock reminded her that she had an appointment with Katherine to try on the blue gown. Accordingly, she walked to the Corning home where her friends awaited her.

"This is the last time you'll come here for a fitting," Helen told Nancy joyously. "Katherine has rented a little shop in the arcade of the Hotel Claymore. After the style show is over, she'll be swamped with orders."

"It worry me," Katherine declared as she brought out the evening dress for Nancy to slip on. "Everyone has been so kind. The shop— Mr. and Mrs. Corning pay the rent."

"Now don't start that all over again," Helen interrupted teasingly. "As soon as you're established, you will be able to repay Dad."

"But if I fail?"

"You won't fail, darling!"

The fitting proceeded, and even the critical Katherine declared that the Renaissance costume could not be improved upon.

"It is perfect," she announced, sitting back on her heels to get a better view of Nancy, who stood before a full-length mirror. "But for your hair you need some touch—a lovely jeweled ornament."

"I never owned one," Nancy replied. "Mrs. Gruen never wanted me to wear fancy jewelry."

"But this is a style show," Helen said quickly. "The costume really requires it."

"I mean a simple old-fashioned ornament, which fit across your hair—so!" Katherine explained, holding a pair of scissors on the Drew girl's head to illustrate.

"Where can we get such a thing?" Nancy asked in perplexity.

"In my country it would have been so easy," declared Katherine. "Here I do not know your shops."

"I understand what you want, but I doubt that such an ornament can be bought," Nancy said. "It's possible Mr. Faber might have one, though."

After leaving the house, she tried several stores in a vain attempt to purchase the hair ornament. Next she called upon Mr. Faber, but before explaining her errand, she told him that Mrs. Alexandra's grandson had been found.

"Ah, this is the happiest day of my life," the old man beamed. "Always I have prayed that Michael would be returned to his grandmother. Ask any favor, and I shall grant it."

Nancy laughingly told of her need for a special hair ornament. Immediately the antique dealer searched the shelves of his little shop, and even examined the contents of a bulky box he kept in the safe.

"Oh, don't put yourself to so much trouble," Nancy protested at last. "I'll find one somewhere else."

Mr. Faber pondered a moment. Then his wrinkled face brightened with an idea.

"You wait!" he commanded, moving to his desk. "I will write a note for you to take to Mrs. Alexandra. She has just the piece you want, and will lend it to you."

Nancy protested that she could not ask such a favor, but the shopkeeper paid no heed to her words. He wrote the message, and sealed the envelope with his signet ring.

"Deliver this to Mrs. Alexandra," he urged. "A hair ornament is a trifle to a woman of her position. And did you not return her long lost grandson?"

Somewhat diffidently, Nancy carried the message the following afternoon to the queen mother. The kindly woman read it, smiled, and then spoke rapidly to Anna in her native tongue. The servant vanished, to reappear a few minutes later with a sparkling ornament on a purple velvet cushion.

Nancy drew in her breath. She had not expected anything so beautiful. The stones, rubies and diamonds, twinkled brilliantly.

"It is yours to keep," smiled Mrs. Alexandra. "Later I hope to offer a more suitable present as a token of my deep gratitude."

Words failed Nancy. She stammered that she could not accept such a valuable gift. Not until she saw that her refusal was offending the woman did she reluctantly agree to wear the ornament in the fashion show.

"Even so, I cannot keep the piece," she insisted. "Immediately after the final performance on Saturday night I shall return it."

"As you wish, my dear," Mrs. Alexandra consented with a sigh. "I must find some other way to express my appreciation."

While Anna wrapped the bright hair ornament, Mrs. Alexandra eagerly talked of her grandson. Nancy must view the splendid room that had been prepared for him. When had the girl last seen the young man? What were his words when he learned that he was to be restored to his loving grandmother?

Nancy neatly side-stepped the questions. She was far too kind to tell her true impression. Early that morning she had talked with Francis Baum by telephone, and he had seemed more interested in what his grandmother could do for him than in anything else. Actually he had asked how much she thought the "old lady" was worth.

"I am sure your grandson should be very happy here," she replied. "You have overlooked nothing for his comfort."

"Everything is nearly ready now for his arrival. Anna and I will welcome him tomorrow night with a grand dinner to celebrate the event. Your own invitation is in the mail."

Nancy gazed about the living room with troubled eyes. A few of the art treasures had been put away, but a great many pieces remained. Fragile glass stood on small antique tables. The slightest push against them would cause disaster.

"I can't help wondering what Mr. Baum's police dog will do to this room," she remarked significantly.

"My grandson has a dog?" Mrs. Alexandra asked in consternation.

"Indeed, he has. And it isn't very well

trained. Gallops around, knocking over things and playing pranks.''

"Oh, dear, I detest dogs, especially large ones. What shall I do about it?''

"Why not advise Mr. Baum to leave his pet behind?''

"Would he not be offended?'' his grand-mother questioned anxiously. "Michael means everything to me——''

"I'll handle the matter for you, if I may,'' Nancy offered. "I am certain I can induce your grandson to give up his dog.''

"Oh, thank you so much,'' the elderly lady said in gratitude.

The conversation shifted to another topic, that of Mr. Faber. Mrs. Alexandra told Nancy that the shop owner's grandfather had been a distinguished personage in her country.

"Not only was he a great jeweler, but he perfected a formula for non-crackable enamel.''

"But I thought no such formula exists to-day!'' Nancy exclaimed, astonished.

"Unfortunately the formula was lost. You must ask Mr. Faber to tell you all about it some time.''

Mrs. Alexandra suddenly seemed weary. She closed her eyes and stopped speaking. Nancy had intended to speak of the singing nightingale and his strange song, but decided not to do so now.

Anna's appearance with the jeweled hair or-nament was a signal for the girl to say good-by. The maid apologized for having had to put the

box in a plain brown bag. Nancy took the bag,
and left the house.

"I am afraid Mrs. Alexandra will be disappointed when she meets her grandson," she reflected as she started slowly toward home.
"But at least she'll not have to endure the dog.
I'll tell Francis Baum flatly that he must get
rid of the animal."

So intent was Nancy upon how she would
deal with the young man that she had failed to
observe a shadowy figure watching her from
around the corner of the house. He glued his
eyes upon the girl, nodding in satisfaction at
sight of the paper bag.

Waiting until she had gone a short distance
down the street, he stealthily followed Nancy.

CHAPTER X

A Snatched Package

UNAWARE that she was being followed, Nancy walked on, deep in thought. Presently she approached a lonely section of the street, where there was an old cemetery with a high, vine-covered wall. No one was in sight, except the lone man and the unsuspecting girl toward whom he drew closer.

Suddenly the tires of a speeding automobile screeched on the pavement. Startled, Nancy turned her head to see why the driver of the car had stopped so abruptly. As she stared at a gray coupé which had pulled up at the curb, the man behind her brushed past. He jostled the girl's arm, knocking the brown bag from her hand.

"Excuse me," he muttered, keeping his head down and his face turned.

Nancy feared for a moment that he meant to steal the precious package, but the man went on hurriedly. The driver of the gray coupé alighted, and politely picked it up for her.

"Don't you remember me?" he asked as he returned the bag. "Why, I'm an old friend!"

"You're Mr. Dorrance," Nancy said.

"Right you are. Didn't even have to wave a handkerchief, did I?"

"Not this time. That pickpocket wouldn't be likely to speak to me."

"How about a lift home?" the man offered. "I'm going your way."

"No, thank you," Nancy politely declined the invitation. "I prefer to walk."

She never accepted rides from persons she did not know well. Nancy had met David Dorrance in a most informal way, and she had no desire to become better acquainted with him.

"Suit yourself," the man shrugged his shoulders. "Well, see you later!"

Jumping into the coupé, he quickly drove away.

Nancy reached home without further incident. Finding Mrs. Gruen in the kitchen, she told her about borrowing the diamond and ruby piece from Mrs. Alexandra.

"It's beautiful," she declared, opening the bag. "Why, it's not here!"

Dumbfounded, Nancy drew forth a dirt-covered stone.

"The ornament has been stolen!" she cried, collapsing into a chair. "I've been tricked!"

"How dreadful!" said the housekeeper.

The loss made Nancy ill. She knew that the piece had been inside the bag when she had left Mrs. Alexandra's home. A daring thief either had substituted another bag, or else slipped the stone inside this one in place of the small jewel case.

"It was either David Dorrance or that man who brushed against me!" she thought angrily. "They both had a chance to do it!"

Nancy was inclined to believe that the act had been committed by the unknown person, who no doubt knew what she was carrying. She recalled how he had shielded his face as he brushed past her.

"I dread telling Mrs. Alexandra," the girl groaned. "Why, that ornament must have cost a small fortune!"

"You never should have borrowed such an expensive headdress," chided the housekeeper. "If it really has been stolen, there's nothing you can do except offer to pay Mrs Alexandra for the loss."

"I can notify the police at least!"

Spurred to action, Nancy ran to the telephone. Her complaint was duly recorded by the lieutenant on duty. He assured her they would do what they could. However, without a description of the thief there seemed scant likelihood that he could be apprehended.

"Now the next thing you must do is report the loss to Mrs. Alexandra," urged the housekeeper as Nancy left the telephone.

"I just hate to!"

"You must do it at once, Nancy."

"I know," the girl returned despairingly. "I'll go now, but it is the most disagreeable task I've ever had in my life."

Leaden feet carried her once more to the home of Mrs. Alexandra. While the woman listened in amazement, Nancy told how the ornament had been taken from her.

"The piece did have great value," the owner acknowledged. "A thief must have seen Anna put it into the bag. No doubt he watched her through the window."

Nancy's spirits dropped even lower, for she was afraid she might never be able to repay the great loss. At that moment Anna came into the room. Her mistress told her what had happened.

"Madame Marie," she said quickly, "the stolen ornament was not the genuine one."

"You wrapped up the imitation headdress?" the elderly lady cried in delight. "The one Mr. Faber sold to me before he found the original family piece?"

"Yes, Madame."

"Anna, you are the brightest of all my jewels!" the gracious lady praised her servant. "How many times you have saved me from my own folly."

Nancy felt so grateful that she could have hugged the taciturn Anna.

"I am happy that the real ornament is safe," Mrs. Alexandra declared. "Since I meant you to have the genuine one, Nancy, you may take it now if you wish."

"And risk another theft? Oh, no!"

"Then Anna and I will keep the headdress for you until Thursday, if you prefer."

"That will suit me much better," Nancy declared as she arose to leave. "And when I come for it, I may bring a bodyguard! I don't propose to be caught napping again.''

Dinner was ready by the time the girl reached her own home. Mrs. Gruen had prepared an excellent meal, but for some reason Carson Drew ate very little.

''What's wrong, Dad?'' Nancy inquired, glancing up from her plate. ''Aren't you feeling well?''

''Oh, I'm all right.''

''Then you're worried. Is it about that wallet you lost?''

''Well, I had hoped it would be returned,'' the lawyer admitted. ''At least the papers in it.''

''You ran a newspaper advertisement, didn't you?''

''Yes, I offered a twenty-five dollar reward and no questions asked. Nothing came of it.''

''I've had no luck in tracing the pickpocket, either,'' Nancy said, sighing.

''Right now I am more concerned about another matter,'' continued her father. ''Old Mrs. Jason, the lady who allowed the Boys Club the use of her property without charge, died a few weeks ago.''

''Didn't she will the club building to the boys?''

''I am sure she intended to, Nancy, but no will has turned up. The heirs are out-of-town people. They have no interest in River Heights, and insist that the property be sold.''

''Oh, that seems unfair! Especially when

the poor boys went to so much trouble to fix up
the club rooms."

"All their work will be lost," Mr. Drew said
gloomily.

"Can't you do anything about it?"

"The heirs are within their rights, Nancy.
I talked with Judge Harland today. Neither
of us can see any way to save the property."

At that moment the discussion was interrupted by the ringing of the doorbell. Guess-
ing that it was for her, Nancy ran to see. As she
opened the door, a young man, broad of shoulder, heavily tanned, clicked his heels sharply
and saluted.

"Ned Nickerson!" Nancy cried jubilantly.
"When did you breeze into town?"

"About two hours ago," he laughed, seizing
her hand. "I just finished my job as swimming
coach at that boys camp."

Nancy and Ned were friends of long standing. They enjoyed the same things and frequently were seen together at parties. Although the girl had many other admirers, she
frankly admitted to herself that Ned was her
favorite.

"What's on your calendar for tonight?" he
asked, as they sat together on the porch swing.

"I have a date," Nancy said with genuine
regret. "Why didn't you warn me you were
coming home?"

"How about tomorrow night?"

"A Mrs. Alexandra is giving a grand dinner
party. Dad and I are to take a Francis Baum

to her home for the first time. It's thrilling, Ned! He's supposed to be a missing prince——"

"Wish he'd stay missing," Ned muttered darkly. "Well, how about tomorrow afternoon?"

"I'll be free between three and five o'clock. I'll go out with you, if you'll guarantee to get me home in time to dress for the dinner party."

"All right, we'll take in the carnival," Ned said, none too well pleased. "Everything from fortunetelling to the roller coaster."

The following afternoon they arrived at the carnival grounds. Mingling with the crowd, they wandered about, enjoying the various amusements. They even rode on the merry-go-round, and raced in miniature automobiles.

Finally Ned bought tickets for the roller coaster. As the car dashed madly down into each trellis-work valley, Nancy held her breath and clung to Ned. So thoroughly did the young man enjoy this that he suggested a second ride.

"No, let's try something else," Nancy pleaded. "How about the ferris wheel?"

"Too tame."

"After that wild ride I crave something mild."

"Then up we go," Ned gave in reluctantly.

He bought tickets, and they sat down in one of the cages. Soon the giant wheel began to turn. It moved very slowly. The motor which rotated it made a loud, racking noise.

"Terrible!" pronounced Ned. "Sounds as if it were going to fall to pieces!"

"It's poky, too," Nancy admitted. "Oh, well, the torture won't last long."

As she spoke, the ferris wheel came to a grinding halt. The cage in which Nancy and Ned were seated remained stationary at the very top. Minutes elapsed, and the wheel did not start again.

"What's the matter with this old rattle-trap?" Ned demanded, peering over the side.

Below he could see two men working over the machinery. Persons in the lower cages close to the ground were being helped out.

"Leaping catfish!" Ned exclaimed. "We're stuck up here!"

"They'll soon have us down," Nancy said, undismayed. "In the meantime, let's enjoy the view."

"The sun's hot and I'm thirsty."

"We might ask one of the men to pass us up some cool drinks," Nancy giggled.

"Now that's a real idea," Ned praised her cheerfully. "I'll go to work on it."

He called to the men below, suggesting that they pass up both food and drink by means of long poles, which could be handed from car to car. Other trapped passengers took up the cry.

At first the request was looked upon as a joke, but as time wore on and the wheel still did not move, Ned asked a second time. Soon the owners were so beset by those above them that to stop the clamor they did as requested.

"Still enjoying the view?" Ned teased Nancy after an hour had elapsed.

"It's getting a bit monotonous." The girl shifted into a more comfortable position as she glanced at her wrist watch. "If I don't get home soon, I'll be late for Mrs. Alexandra's dinner."

"That's so," Ned agreed soberly. "Wish I could do something."

"I asked Francis Baum to come to our house at six-thirty," Nancy resumed restlessly. "Katherine Kovna has been invited, too," she added, and went on to tell him about the designer.

"I guess the workmen expect to get the levers fixed any minute now," Ned said a little later to encourage her. "Cheer up!"

Nancy settled back into her seat again, forcing herself to remain calm. Her gaze roved to a group of curious merrymakers who had gathered some distance away to stare at the motionless ferris wheel. As she idly watched, a small man, who walked with quick, short steps, edged close to another man. Deftly he removed a wallet from the hip pocket of the unsuspecting victim. Unobserved by those about him, he turned to slip away in the crowd.

"Ned!" Nancy clutched his hand. "I just saw a pickpocket take a man's wallet! Oh, we must do something!"

"What can we do?"

Together they shouted, trying to attract the attention of someone on the ground. Other trapped passengers were making so much noise that no one paid any heed to them.

"It's no use now," Nancy said at last. "The pickpocket is gone, and we'll probably be here forever!"

Barely had she spoken than the sleeping ferris wheel began to move. The cars jerked violently.

"Here we go!" exclaimed Ned jubilantly.

The next instant the cages raced downward at a breath-taking speed. The ferris wheel was completely out of control!

CHAPTER XI

GUESTS OF HONOR

THE ferris wheel made a complete revolution, stopping with a terrific jerk. Once more the car in which Ned and Nancy were imprisoned stopped at the top.

"Oh, that was awful!" the girl cried.

In the cage beneath them, two little girls began to whimper with fear. The younger child stood up and started to unfasten the safety bar.

"I'm going to jump out!" she screamed hysterically. "I won't stay on this horrible ferris wheel another minute!"

Nancy, thoroughly alarmed, leaned far over. She spoke to the frightened children soothingly. Ned assured them that the machine soon would be repaired.

"Just see!" Nancy said cheerfully. "A photographer has come to take your picture. He's pointing his camera directly at you."

The prospect of having their pictures taken on the ferris wheel took the children's minds off their predicament. They sat down again and even smiled as the shutter clicked. Ned and Nancy pulled themselves back in their cage, so that they would not be snapped.

A moment later the ferris wheel began to revolve. Everyone sat tense, fearful of another

84

wild ride. But this time the cages moved only
a few feet at a time, and one by one the passengers emerged from them.

"At last!" breathed Nancy, as she and Ned
were released. "If we hurry, I can still reach
home in time to dress and not be late to dinner."

"Just a minute!" interposed the photographer, focusing his camera.

"We don't want our pictures taken," refused Ned, deliberately turning his back.

The insistent man ran around in front of the
couple. Before the girl could duck her head, he
had snapped the picture.

"The nerve of that fellow!" Ned exclaimed
angrily. "I'd like to punch him in the nose!"

"Another time, if you don't mind," Nancy
laughed to cover her irritation. "I really must
get home!"

Hailing a taxi, the couple soon were on their
way to the Drew house.

"I wish you had been invited to the dinner,
Ned," his companion said regretfully, as she
bade him good-by at the door.

"Oh, I can bear up," the youth chuckled.
"All I ask is that you don't pay too much attention to that prince fellow."

"I hope he has arrived," Nancy said anxiously. "It's really late."

A taxicab drew up near-by. Katherine
Kovna, dressed in a white evening gown with
matching coat and beaded bag, alighted at the
curb. She was alone, for Helen Corning, al-

though invited to the dinner, had been unable to accept.

"Am I early?" Katherine inquired.

"You're exactly on time," Nancy replied. "I am the offender. But it won't take me long to get ready."

Explaining briefly what had occurred, she and Katherine entered the house. Her father was just coming down the stairway, very handsome in his summer dress suit.

"Nancy, what delayed you?" he reproved her mildly. "Usually I am the one who holds up the show!"

Again Nancy offered her excuses. Mrs. Gruen, entering from another room, urged her to hurry.

"Your clothes are ready. I've pressed your evening dress," she told the girl.

"Francis Baum isn't here?" Nancy asked, as she took the stairs two steps at a time.

"Not yet," her father answered. "He'll probably be along in a minute or two."

Nancy took a shower and dressed in record time. As she surveyed herself in a long mirror, she decided that the red and white gown, with black velvet trimming, really was attractive. She hastened downstairs.

"Baum hasn't arrived," Mr. Drew said, glancing at his watch. "Are you sure he understood he was to come to our house, Nancy?"

"Oh, yes, Dad. I telephoned him this morning to make certain. I was afraid he might forget to wear evening clothes."

"Well, something has delayed him. Unless we start for the Alexandra home immediately, we'll be late."

Mrs. Gruen, who stood at the front door, called out, "There's someone coming down the street. He's dressed in sports clothes, though."

"Then it couldn't be Mr. Baum," Nancy replied.

"All the same, it looks like him. He has a suitcase and a big police dog!"

"A dog!" Nancy's face darkened. "I distinctly told him he was not to bring that animal!"

Darting to the window, she saw that the young man who approached was indeed Francis Baum. She was very annoyed at his actions.

"Guess I'm a little late," the young man said without concern, but made no excuse for his attire.

"Didn't you understand that we were to dress in evening clothes?" Mr. Drew inquired.

"Yes, but I didn't have time to bother."

Nancy felt that he might have shown more desire to please his grandmother on their first meeting. He surely had enough money to have rented the proper clothes, if he didn't own them.

"Why did you bring the dog?" she asked.

"Can't I take him along?"

"We went through that before, Mr. Baum."

"Well, then I'll have to leave him here," the young man shrugged.

"Here?" inquired Hannah Gruen with a rising accent.

"Just overnight. He's harmless—won't make a bit of trouble."

"I'll not be here to look after him," the housekeeper said coldly. "I intend to go to a movie."

"Oh, he'll stay in the yard," Francis Baum said carelessly. "I'll tie him by the garage."

The hour was so late that no other disposition could be made of the dog. Mr. Baum seemed unaware that he had caused the slightest inconvenience. As the invited guests taxied to the Alexandra home, he annoyed Nancy and Katherine with profuse compliments regarding their appearance.

"I suppose you're eager to see your grandmother," Mr. Drew remarked, studying the young man curiously.

"Oh, sure," he replied, but his tone lacked warmth. "What's she like?"

"Decidedly formal," Nancy warned him severely.

"Maybe she won't let me eat with you in these clothes," he grinned. "But she'll soon like me," he added confidently.

Nancy avoided looking at her father and Katherine. They all felt sick at heart, knowing that Mrs. Alexandra could not fail to be disappointed upon meeting her grandson.

The taxi halted in front of the house, which

glowed with lights. Mr. Drew paid the driver
and followed the others to the door. Almost
at once it was opened by a butler engaged for
the evening.

As Mr. Drew handed over his hat, his gaze
wandered to an unusual card tray on the hall
table. Constructed of copper, it was decorated
with colored bits of enamel in a flower and leaf
design.

"There is a sample of wonderful old enamel
work," he whispered to Nancy. "I suppose
Faber's father made it."

"You'll see many other treasures, unless
Mrs. Alexandra has put them away," she replied in a low tone.

Anna came to escort the girls upstairs, and
helped them remove their wraps. Excitedly
they returned to the first floor and entered the
living room.

There Mrs. Alexandra, gowned in rich ma-
roon velvet trimmed with real lace, greeted her
guests. Her eyes were moist as she kissed
Francis Baum on either cheek. If his appearance startled her, she did not disclose it.

"Michael," she said tenderly, leading him to
a sofa, "you cannot understand what this hour
means to me. For years I have prayed that
we would be reunited."

"I'm glad to know you," he replied. "But
I thought my name was Francis. I've always
been called that. Guess Mom was afraid to call
me Michael."

Nancy thought she detected a slight start on

the part of her hostess. It seemed strange that his nurse, even though a foster mother, would have had a royal child call her "Mom."

"Michael Alexandra is your true name," the queen mother explained. "Do you recall anything of life at the palace?"

Francis squirmed uncomfortably. "I remember seeing some swell parades," he volunteered. "That's about all."

An awkward pause followed. It was broken by the butler announcing dinner. As the double doors of the dining room were opened, Nancy drew in her breath. Never had she seen such a beautiful table setting. Orchids formed the centerpiece, the cloth was made of rare lace, and at each place was a name card held in a silver basket.

Francis Baum found his chair at once and sat down without waiting for the others. To cover his mistake, Mrs. Alexandra quickly seated herself. It was evident to everyone that she meant to spare her grandson embarrassment.

The first course—there were eight to follow —was a mixture of rare fruits served in fragile handblown glass cups. The service plates were of rich dark blue and gold, with hand-painted bouquets. The handles of the knives and forks were inlaid with mother-of-pearl.

Nancy and Katherine were so impressed by the splendor that they felt as if they were dining in fairyland. A glance at Francis Baum, however, sufficed to bring them to earth with a rude jolt. The young man did his best to eat properly, but made one mistake after another, both in his table manners and in his attempt at conversation.

"He certainly has forgotten everything he ever was taught," thought Nancy. "Poor Mrs. Alexandra. She looked forward to this meeting with such high hopes."

Dessert was served on dainty plates of salmon and gold. Their decorations of enamel were so unusual that Mr. Drew could not refrain from admiring the work.

"It is indeed remarkable," Mrs. Alexandra admitted, pleased by his interest. "At one time, only the ladies of the court had dessert served on these plates," she smiled, "but now I am sharing this secret with you gentlemen."

As the conversation became merry, Francis Baum was silent. At last his grandmother sought to draw him into it once more.

"Michael dear, do tell us something of your life here in America," she urged kindly. "I fear you have had a very hard time."

"Nothing to tell," he mumbled, avoiding her gaze. "After my foster mother died, I had to shift for myself. I didn't have a chance to get much education—too busy working."

"You shall have an opportunity to learn now, Michael. You'll have a tutor."

"I'll need to find out how to handle myself in society," the young man admitted. "You can teach me the ropes yourself, though, can't you?"

Mrs. Alexandra looked slightly distressed because of the crude expression. The next instant she smiled. Arising, she signified that the long dinner had ended.

The guests returned to the living room, from which many art treasures had been removed. The Easter egg, too, had disappeared, so she did not suggest that her father be given an opportunity to hear the nightingale's song.

Realizing that Mrs. Alexandra no doubt wished to be alone with her grandson, the guests soon offered excuses for leaving. Francis Baum followed Nancy into the hall, and managed to whisper in her ear:

"How about you and me having a date one of these nights?"

"Thank you, I'll be very busy—for some time," Nancy declined.

"Oh, come on. Do it as a favor to my grandmother."

Nancy was glad that Mrs. Alexandra's appearance at that moment made it unnecessary for her to reply. The Drews and Katherine departed, leaving Baum in his new home.

"I never met a less attractive young man," she confessed to her father, as they motored home after taking Katherine to the Corning residence. "How could he behave as he did?"

"Because he knew no better, Nancy."

"It's difficult to believe that he's of royal blood. If his credentials hadn't been excellent, I should be inclined to think he's an impostor."

"Training may make young Baum into a new

person,'' declared Mr. Drew. "Let's hope so, at least.''

The taxi halted at their home. Nancy and her father alighted. The windows in the house were dark, evidence that Mrs. Gruen had not returned from the theater.

As Mr. Drew neared the front porch, he was startled to hear an angry growl. From the steps Francis Baum's police dog leaped at him.

"How did that animal get loose?'' he muttered impatiently.

The dog crouched as if to leap upon Nancy and her father. They spoke soothingly to him, but to no avail.

"Let's try the back door,'' she suggested.

The annoying beast followed them to the rear of the house. He became increasingly unfriendly, and would not let them come within several yards of either porch.

"What shall we do, Dad?''

"It's too late to telephone the dog warden, and it would be too bad to ask the police to shoot the animal,'' her father replied.

"We can't stay outdoors all night!'' said Nancy.

Mr. Drew picked up a stout stick.

"You'll be bitten!'' Nancy pleaded, seizing his arm. "There must be some other way to take care of this!''

Mr. Drew nodded grimly.

"I know what we'll do,'' he said with satisfaction. "Just follow me, Nancy.''

CHAPTER XII

A Dog on Guard

Mr. Drew led the way to the home of a friend across the street. Grimly he told Nancy that he proposed to telephone Francis Baum and ask him to come for his dog.

"That's a good idea," she agreed. "I bet he won't want to do it, though!"

The owner of the animal was anything but cooperative. He tried to avoid making the trip, but when Mr. Drew remained firm, he finally said he supposed he would have to come.

"Who does that fellow think he is, anyway?" the lawyer demanded, as he sat down on the neighbor's porch steps to await the man.

"Merely a prince," Nancy giggled. "Since he has the title, perhaps he feels he should act the part."

"Putting other people to a lot of trouble is anything but princely!" declared her father. "Why don't you wait inside, Nancy?" he suggested after a few minutes. "I'll stay here and watch for Baum."

"No, I wouldn't desert you," she laughed, snuggling close to his arm. "His Royal Highness will arrive soon."

Minutes elapsed and Mr. Drew became more

impatient. Again he tried to get into the house, but the dog appeared to be more ferocious than ever, so he returned to the porch across the street. After nearly an hour had gone by, he announced that he would telephone again to the young man. At that instant a taxicab rolled down the street and stopped.

"There he is now!" the lawyer muttered. "It's about time, too!"

Instead of apologizing for the trouble he had caused, Francis Baum adopted the attitude that he had been imposed upon.

"I was just ready to go to bed when you telephoned," he complained to Mr. Drew. "Couldn't you handle the dog without bothering me?"

"I could have turned him over to the police," the lawyer retorted testily. "They probably would have shot him."

Francis Baum called the dog, who responded readily to his master. He loaded the oversized animal into the cab, and left without a word of apology.

"Dad, I'm afraid you weren't very polite to the prince," Nancy said teasingly. "Not that he deserved any better treatment."

"I've had enough of that young man," Mr. Drew replied. "In fact, if I never meet him again, I will be pleased."

Nancy and her father let themselves into the house.

"Think I'll turn in immediately," Mr. Drew yawned. "I've had a big day."

"So have I," added his daughter wearily. "Those hours spent on the ferris wheel seemed to wear me out."

Going at once to her room, she tumbled into bed and did not even hear Mrs. Gruen, who arrived only a few minutes later. She slept until nine o'clock the next morning, when the housekeeper entered the bedroom.

"Nancy," the woman began, observing that the girl had awakened, "I can't imagine why you allowed those newspapermen to take your picture and write you up as a heroine!"

"What's that?" The girl rubbed her eyes and sat up in bed.

"Just look at the front page of this morning's paper," the housekeeper said, handing it to the girl.

The *River Heights Times* carried a two-column picture of Nancy and Ned, their heads lowered, as they obviously fled from photographers. A headline proclaimed:

HEROINE AVOIDS CAMERA AFTER SAVING CHILDREN

The accompanying article offered a highly colored account of how she had kept the excited youngsters from leaping out of the ferris wheel.

"How annoying!" Nancy exclaimed. "With the Fashion Show starting Thursday, people will think I am trying to get some publicity for myself."

"Not those who know you," Mrs. Gruen soothed her. "At any rate, since the story is true, you can't ask for a denial."

With the show almost at hand, Nancy had no time to think more about the incident. Immediately after breakfast she attended a rehearsal held at the Woman's Club. Many gorgeous costumes, which the other models were to wear, were on display.

"There's not an entry to compare with the Kovna-Drew combination," Helen Corning assured the girls confidently. "Don't you two think you will win first prize?"

Nancy had answered the question many times. "I hope so," she replied, "but the competition will be keen."

Although Katherine had declared the Renaissance-designed gown finished, she kept adding final touches.

"Every detail must be—perfect," she explained. "I think I make loops of the dress material to swing gracefully from the back of your hair."

"I'll feel like a young queen!" chuckled Nancy. "I only hope I can do the gown justice."

To complete the elaborate headdress, Katherine had need of the ornament which Mrs. Alexandra had promised to lend. Accordingly, Nancy, accompanied by Bess and George, set off to get it.

"We'll see that no wicked pickpocket overpowers you this time," George promised

"Bess and I will serve as your bodyguards."

"See you at the picnic this noon," said Nancy.

"It is sweet of Helen to give it for me," said Katherine with a smile.

En route to Mrs. Alexandra's home, the girls passed Mr. Faber's shop and paused to say hello. The previous day he had been told how the imitation ruby and diamond piece had been snatched from Nancy. She was startled to see that same glittering bit of jewelry lying on one of his show counters.

"Why, Mr. Faber, where did you get this?" she asked in astonishment.

"From a pawnbroker," the old man chuckled. "The imitation piece turned up in the hands of a dealer in town."

"Then the fellow who snatched it from me must have pawned it!"

"Yes, and he got only two dollars for his trouble! See, I return your property."

Smiling, Mr. Faber placed the hair ornament in a padded case and gave it to Nancy. He would not allow her to pay him.

"You are a friend of Mrs. Alexandra," he said quietly. "We both owe you a great favor."

With the imitation ornament once more in her possession, Nancy remarked that it would not be necessary for her to borrow the original from Mrs. Alexandra.

"You make a mistake if you do not wear the

genuine piece," Mr. Faber advised. "This one looks very cheap in comparison."

"I'll decide later," Nancy replied, still not convinced.

The girls bade the man a good day and continued their walk to Mrs. Alexandra's house.

"I am glad for your sake," the woman smiled when Nancy told her that the headdress had been recovered, "but really it did not matter."

The girls had hoped to talk with her alone, so they were disappointed to find Francis Baum there. He explained that he had given up his job, and now had much leisure time.

"It's not fitting for a prince to stand behind a counter," he said loftily. "Grandmother says I did the right thing to give up my work."

"Michael will need all his time for his studies," Mrs. Alexandra added. "I hope to engage a tutor for him within a few days."

"No hurry about it," the young man interposed. "I want to have a good time for awhile. Remember, I've been working all my life."

Bess and George noticed that many art treasures had been removed from the living room. Nancy had neglected to tell them that Anna had put away the various objects, until the women should become better acquainted with the newcomer in their home.

"What became of the little Easter egg?" Bess asked, never dreaming that she was giving away a secret.

Francis Baum roused himself to alert atten tion.

"Easter egg?" he demanded. "What's that, Grandmother?"

"Merely one of the things I brought with me when I came to this country."

"Let's see what it's like."

Mrs. Alexandra ordered Anna to bring the little treasure. The servant obeyed reluctantly.

Francis Baum's eyes brightened at sight of the gold-encrusted case. He raised the lid. Beholding the nightingale, he astonished everyone by asking if it could sing.

"Then you too know the secret!" Mrs. Alexandra exclaimed.

"My foster mother once told me something about it," the young man replied.

She took the beautiful ornament from him. At the touch of her finger the nightingale sang his little song. Nancy waited to see if the young man would give any hint that he understood the words. He gave no sign that he did.

"How many languages do you speak?" she asked him after a moment.

"Only English," he replied. "That's good enough for me. My foster mother was afraid we'd get in trouble if we spoke anything else."

Mrs. Alexandra told the story of her escape from her country, much the same as Nancy had heard it from old Mr. Faber.

"Michael dear, what did your nurse tell you about the nightingale?" she asked at length.

"Just about what you've told me," he answered.

"Have you no recollections of your early childhood?" she prodded him.

"I can remember parades and soldiers with plumes on their helmets."

"Nothing else?"

"We've gone into that so many times," Michael said wearily. "Why do you keep asking me?"

As if to escape further questioning, the young man arose. Saying that he would bring in a cold drink of fruit juice, which Anna had prepared, he hurriedly left the room.

Nancy waited a moment to be certain that the grandson was well beyond hearing. Then she told Mrs. Alexandra that Katherine thought the nightingale might be saying in her native tongue, "Clue in Jewel Box."

The ex-queen touched the secret spring several times. Finally she admitted that the little bird might be trying to convey such a message.

"Do you know what it means?" asked Nancy, leaning forward eagerly.

Before Mrs. Alexandra could reply, those in the living room were startled by a loud crash. From the kitchen Anna's voice was raised in fright and anger.

"Oh, Michael!" they heard her wail, "what have you done now?"

CHAPTER XIII

Overboard!

Mrs. Alexandra and the three girls, alarmed by Anna's cries, hastened to the kitchen. On the floor lay a porcelain bowl which had broken into a dozen pieces.

"Madame Marie, it was not my fault!" the servant said, her dark eyes fastening accusingly on Michael.

"No, blame me!" he retorted sharply. "Sure, I did it. Brushed against it by accident. Why so much fuss over an old cracked bowl?"

"Old? Cracked?" Anna murmured, her voice rising. "That lovely porcelain cannot be replaced. It was given to Madame by the king."

"There, Anna, please say no more," Mrs. Alexandra interrupted. "It was an accident. After all, my grandson is far more precious to me than the most valuable piece of porcelain in the world."

"That's the way to talk, Grandmother!" nodded Michael. "Who's going to worry about an old bowl? I'll get you another one."

It was easy to see that Mrs. Alexandra felt deeply distressed. Nevertheless, she passed the matter off with regal composure. Nancy thought that the incident had wearied the deli-

cate woman, so she did not again bring up the
nightingale's mysterious reference to a jewel
box.

"We must leave now," she said consider-
ately. "May I take this hair ornament I borrowed before?"

To her dismay, Mrs. Alexandra asked Anna
to bring the genuine piece.

"You must wear this in the Fashion Show,"
she insisted. "It was never my intention to
offer you an imitation."

Nancy did not want to offend the woman a
second time, yet she was fearful that something
would happen to the ruby and diamond tiara-
like headdress.

"I'm really afraid to borrow it," she declared dubiously.

"Do take it to please me," Mrs. Alexandra
urged. "I assume all responsibility."

Nancy thanked the woman, and with her
chums left the house. They carried the precious package at once to Katherine.

"Ah, it will set off the Renaissance costume!" the designer approved in delight.
"For safekeeping, I ask Helen's father to put
the ornament in his strongbox!"

Nancy felt relieved. She started for home
in a happy mood to dress for the picnic. She
decided to stop at police headquarters and in-
quire if any petty thieves had been captured
during the past twenty-four hours. She was
told by the Chief that a man had just been
brought in for questioning.

"May I see him?" the girl requested.

"Glad to have you," the officer replied.

Well acquainted with both Nancy and her father, he frequently received useful clues and tips from them. In fact, so many cases had the Drew girl solved that he jokingly declared Nancy to be an unofficial member of his staff!

The man who had been captured was placed in a line-up with other suspects. Nancy studied each person carefully as he stood on a platform under a powerful light. The short, wiry pickpocket she had hoped to identify was not in the group.

"Sorry," she said regretfully. "I've never seen any of these prisoners before."

As Nancy was about to leave, an irate man burst into the courtroom.

"You policemen are a bunch of thickheads!" he fairly shouted. "Here I've paid city taxes for twelve years, and what do I get in return? Nothing! When I need a policeman, I can't find one! And when I finally get one, he arrests the wrong man!"

"If you have a complaint to make, the lieutenant will take it—over at that desk," a sergeant told him coldly.

Calming down a bit, the man directed his remarks to this person. In a bitter voice he revealed that his wallet had been snatched while he was standing in front of a store window.

He had shouted for a policeman. The officer had arrested a man, who immediately estab-

lished his innocence. A short time later the
missing wallet had been found in an alley, its
entire contents gone.

"You can bet the thief had an accomplice,"
the angry victim declared. "When the policeman came on the run, I heard someone in the
crowd whistle as if in warning."

"You did not see the man who whistled?" he
was questioned.

"No, I didn't. But right after that the thief
threw away the pocketbook. Guess he was
afraid of being caught with it."

The lieutenant promised that he would do
what he could, and made a routine report. After the indignant man had left the station, the
officer gazed rather apologetically at Nancy.

"What can we do?" he asked with a shrug.
"Practically no clues. Money can't be traced,
unless the bills have been marked previously."

"A pickpocket has to be caught in the act,
doesn't he?" Nancy inquired thoughtfully.

"Yes, it's about the only way to nab the slippery fellows. They're far too clever to be
caught with any evidence on them."

"Nancy, I believe you'll have to turn your
talents to this case," called the Police Chief
from across the room, a twinkle in his eye.
"How about helping us out?"

"Too busy today," she joked in return.
"Ask me later on, and I may consider it."

Homeward bound, Nancy began to wonder
whether this latest theft had been committed
by the same pickpocket who had stolen her

father's wallet, and who was causing the epidemic of purse snatching in River Heights.

"Somehow I must recover the money for the Boys Club, and the valuable papers Dad lost!" she thought resolutely. "Not this afternoon, though, for I shall be at Helen's picnic for Katherine. But I may be able to pick up a clue on the way!"

The young people were to go by motorboat far up the river to Star Island. The outing promised to be an especially enjoyable one, for Helen had asked only a few intimate friends.

At the appointed hour, Ned Nickerson called for Nancy at her home. Upon reaching the dock, they found that the others had arrived ahead of them. Ned's college roommate, Buck Rodman, escorted Helen. He had invited a friend, Bob Dutton, for Katherine. George Fayne and an athletic young man, Burt Eddleton, had come together, and Bess brought her latest admirer, Dave Evans.

"Everyone is here," Helen declared, counting all of her guests, who numbered twelve altogether. "Shall we start?"

Two motorboats, to be operated by Ned and Buck, had been rented for the outing. The passengers were divided between the crafts, and Buck started off. The ropes of Ned's craft were about to be cast off, when there came a shout from shore.

"Hey, wait a minute!"

Ned throttled the motor, and everyone turned to see who had called.

"Francis Baum!" said Nancy. "Now Michael Alexandra," she added in explanation.

He was coming along the dock, followed by his dog. Thinking that the young man might have a message for Nancy from his grandmother, Ned waited.

"What's up? A picnic?" the prince demanded as he reached the group.

"You guessed it," answered Ned shortly.

"How about taking me along?"

"The boats are filled now. Otherwise——"

"Oh, you can make room for me," Michael insisted, squeezing in between Nancy and Bess.

"Grandmother wants me to get to know people like you," he said airily, casting his eye over the group.

To everyone's irritation the dog also leaped aboard. Before he could be made to lie on the floor, he had put his dirty paws on Bess's white dress, soiling it badly.

"Hey, pitch that beast out on the dock!" Ned ordered. "We're not going to tote him along."

"If you take me, you must take my dog, too," the unwelcome fellow said breezily.

"Don't remember hearing anyone say we were going to take you," Ned muttered under his breath.

Nancy, afraid Mrs. Alexandra might be hurt if she learned the attitude of the girl's friends, nudged Ned, and he became silent. The girl now presented Michael to the group, being careful not to reveal the identity of Mrs. Alexandra, as the ex-queen had requested. Her grandson, however, spoiled everything.

"Why don't you tell your friends I'm really Prince Michael?" he urged. "It's not everybody who has a queen for a grandmother," he laughed.

Those in the group who did not know the story looked at him in amusement. They thought he was joking, and Nancy did not set them straight.

As they edged away from the wharf, a mahogany colored speedboat cruised past slowly. Its driver was a sad-faced young man. A little boy sat beside him. Michael had bent over suddenly to tie his shoestring, and remained in that position an unusually long time.

"Did he do that on purpose because he was afraid of being seen by that other man?" Nancy asked herself. "It certainly looked so. I wonder who he is."

As the trip proceeded, Bess, Ned, and their friends paid scant attention to Michael. They had started singing. Nancy, crowded by the dog, presently climbed over the seat, and perched herself on the afterdeck of the boat.

"Lots of room back here!" she shouted.

The others paid no attention. They continued singing, and did not join her. She became interested in watching the speedboat which was about to pass them again. Not until the channel buoy had been rounded did Bess glance over her shoulder. Then she gave a little scream of terror.

"Stop the boat, Ned! Quickly!"

"What's wrong?" he demanded, throttling down the motor.

"Nancy's gone!" she cried, pointing to the empty deck. "She must have fallen overboard!"

Overboard 109

CHAPTER XIV

NANCY TO THE RESCUE

NED swung the motorboat in a wide arc, while the worried young people stood up to look across the water. They saw a figure swimming some distance away, so the boat was steered in that direction.

"It's Nancy!" cried Bess, pointing. "She's holding up a little boy!"

Another boat also was speeding toward the scene. Ned was the first to reach Nancy, however. Many hands pulled her and the little fellow aboard. Immediately he began to whimper.

"You're all right," Nancy panted, brushing a strand of wet hair from her eyes. "I reached you before anything happened to you."

"I'm cryin' 'cause my new suit is all wet!" the lad replied. "And Mr. Ellington's going to scold me for falling off his boat."

"What happened, Nancy?" Ned asked, as he removed his coat and wrapped it about her shoulders.

The girl pointed to the approaching speed-boat. "This little fellow tumbled from there a few minutes ago. I shouted to you, and then jumped overboard to rescue him."

"We never heard you," replied Ned. "Are you both all right?"

"Just a little moist," Nancy laughed, wringing water from her skirt.

"You weren't swimming long?" Bess asked anxiously.

"No, but it seemed an age. This lad gave me a battle at first."

"I was scared I was going to drown," the boy apologized. "I didn't mean to fight."

"Of course you didn't."

Nancy put the coat Ned had given her on the shivering youngster. She glanced at Michael, expecting him to offer her his sweater, but he made no such move. Instead, he busied himself in the bottom of the boat, apparently holding down his dog, which had become restless from the excitement. The next moment the boat that had lost its young passenger drew alongside.

"That's Mr. Ellington," the boy said, pointing to the handsome young person at the steering wheel. "I bet he's real mad at me!"

The man was far from angry. He was thoroughly frightened to realize by what a narrow margin a tragedy had been averted. Over and over he thanked Nancy for the rescue.

"You had him before I knew he was overboard," he said shakily. "If anything had happened to Jimmie Irving, I don't know how I could have faced his parents," he declared. "He's the only child of the superintendent of the apartment house where I live across the river."

Jimmie was handed over to Mr. Ellington's

boat, and told to "sit still" until shore could be reached. As the two groups separated, Nancy remarked that the sad-faced young man seemed to be a very cultured individual.

"Too stiff to suit me," cut in Michael, although no one had asked his opinion.

"Mr. Ellington, he is talented commercial artist," contributed Katherine, speaking for the first time.

"Then you know him?" Nancy asked eagerly.

Katherine shook her head. "I see some of his drawings. He sell them, I think, to magazines. Helen say he will be at the Fashion Show, and I must make impression on him!"

"What is Mr. Ellington's first name?" Nancy asked.

"I do not know. He sign all his drawings 'R. H. Ellington.' "

During all this conversation Michael had remained silent. Now he deliberately broke in to change the subject. He praised Nancy's swimming, then spoke of his own prowess in the sport. The girl wondered whether in his crude way he was trying to imitate the conversation of those in what he called "society."

"He's certainly making a bad job of it so far," she decided. "Poor Mrs. Alexandra!"

Star Island soon loomed up, and the boat was tied to a dock near a sandy beach. Helen Corning and her crowd already had arrived. All the young men except Michael offered to carry the picnic hampers to a selected spot among the trees.

"Let's go for a swim!" Nancy proposed
gaily. "While we're in the water, perhaps my
clothes will dry."

"The prince will have a chance to show us
his skill," Ned added grimly.

Mrs. Alexandra's grandson smiled in a superior way. "Sorry, I didn't bring a bathing
suit."

"I'll let you have mine," offered Buck.
"We're about the same size."

"No, thank you," the young man declined.
"I never wear anybody else's clothing."

The others felt certain that he was giving
these lame excuses because he was a poor
swimmer. While they bathed in a sheltered
cove, he amused himself by throwing sticks into
the water among them for his dog to retrieve.

"Can't you play that little game somewhere
else?" Ned demanded crossly.

"So sorry," Michael responded, but he kept
on throwing his sticks in the same area.

"I've had my fill of that fellow!" Ned muttered to Buck Rodman. "Unless he starts acting more like a prince should, I'm going to
settle with him!"

"And I'll help you," added the other youth.

Out of earshot of Nancy they formed a plan,
to be put into effect if Michael should annoy
them any more. The young people decided to
dress. The girls were ready first, and began
to set out the lunch at once. Michael took several sandwiches for his dog without permission.

"I wish those boys would hurry," Helen said

after fifteen minutes had gone by, but presently the youths turned up, grins on their faces.

As the food was passed, it became evident that young Alexandra had learned little from his association with his grandmother. He told a couple dull stories, and annoyed Katherine by his attentions.

"Say, Michael," said Ned, addressing him abruptly, "will you do us a favor?"

"What is it?" the young man asked suspiciously.

"Katherine left her coat in the motorboat. Dash down and get it for her," he replied, giving the girl a broad wink.

The young man considered a moment, and then smiled at the girl. "I'll do it for *you*," he said. "But when I get back, I'll expect a reward."

"You'll get it," promised Ned. "Just trot along."

As Michael started toward the beach with his dog, Nancy glanced questioningly at Ned. Instantly the boys arose, and hurriedly stuffed the remaining food into the hampers.

"We pulled the motorboats to another dock," he explained. "Here's where we leave Prince Charming!"

"I wish we dared!" exclaimed Helen. "He has made such a nuisance of himself."

"Come on!" Ned urged, seizing two of the picnic hampers. "A ferryboat touches Star Island every two hours. His Highness can get home on that."

Nancy felt that they should not do this, but she was overruled. Taking care to keep out of sight, the young people slipped down to the dock and boarded the two boats. The roar of the motors brought Michael sprinting madly down the beach.

"Look at him come!" chuckled Ned, steering away from the island. "The prince is better at foot racing than swimming!"

"Hey, wait for me!" shouted the young man. "Don't go off and leave me stranded."

"Can't hear you," called Buck through cupped hands. "Louder!"

Michael shouted again and again. Finally, as the boats sped far away, he slumped down on the beach.

"It was a mean trick—" Nancy began, but Ned interrupted her.

"He deserved it and a lot more. Don't waste any of your sympathy on him. Save it for Mrs. Alexandra."

When the young people reached River Heights, Nancy went home at once to change her clothes. She and Ned spent the evening at a moving picture show.

The next morning Nancy decided to go to see old Mr. Faber. The antique dealer reported that he thought he had found just the right "gentleman's box" for Mr. Drew, and was having it forwarded from New York City.

"I hope your father likes it," he said anxiously to the girl. "Mrs. Alexandra asked me to make a special effort to please him."

"How nice of her!" Nancy exclaimed. "Have you seen her recently?"

"Anna brought a message from her today," the old man explained. "For that matter, Michael also was here early this morning."

"Michael?"

"Yes, he brought me a jewel to sell for Mrs. Alexandra." Mr. Faber's face became troubled. "I gave her the best price I could, but it worries me that she must sell her treasures."

"Maybe Prince Michael is an expensive grandson to own," Ned remarked with a laugh.

"Ah, yes!" Old Faber's head bobbed up and down. "It is a pity Madame can deny him nothing. The young man has proven a bitter disappointment to me."

When Nancy reached home later, Mrs. Gruen told her that an urgent message awaited her.

"Anna has called twice," the housekeeper said. "Mrs. Alexandra has had another attack, apparently brought on by excitement. Anna wants you to come there at once."

"Of course I'll go," Nancy agreed. "I wonder if Michael had anything to do with Mrs. Alexandra's condition?"

A few minutes later at the Downing Street home she voiced the same thought to the troubled Anna.

"I don't see how Michael can be responsible," the servant replied. "He has been away most of the day."

"Yes, I know," Nancy said, hiding a smile.

"I merely thought that his selling the jewel for Mrs. Alexandra may have upset her."

"Michael sold a jewel for Madame Marie?" Anna's eyes opened wide at this bit of news.

"Didn't you know about it?"

"I certainly did not!" Anna returned with displeasure. "If I had known—but then, it is too late now. Madame Marie has spent money most lavishly the past few days."

"Michael isn't here yet?" Nancy asked thoughtfully.

"He came in about ten minutes ago," the woman replied. "He tied up that dog of his, and went off somewhere."

"Without seeing Mrs. Alexandra?"

"Her condition didn't seem to worry him in the least. But then I was not sorry to keep him from the bedroom. Michael was in a dreadful mood."

"Did he tell you what had upset him?"

"Only that some acquaintances of his had left him stranded on an island yesterday. A fisherman took him off in a small boat. He had to row part of the way to shore, and blistered his hands."

"I see," Nancy said, but made no further comment.

"I am glad it happened," returned Anna, her black eyes flashing. "Michael requires many lessons, to my way of thinking."

"May I see Mrs. Alexandra now?" Nancy asked after a moment of silence.

"Yes, come with me."

As the two started upstairs, the dog that had been tied up began to bark. The disturbance was so loud that Nancy and Anna hastened to a window to see what could be wrong. To their dismay, the huge animal had broken his rope, and was attacking the postman.

"Oh! Oh!" moaned Anna, covering her eyes.

Nancy ran out the door, determined to help the unfortunate mailman. Her eye fell on a whip, which hung from a nail on the porch. Seizing it, she tried to lash at the dog.

"Run!" she shouted to the postman. "Now's your chance!"

He scrambled onto the porch, his uniform ripped from the knees down.

"Look out yourself!" he warned the courageous girl.

"I'm sure the dog knows me by this time," she replied. He won't——"

Nancy whirled around and faced the animal. But he did not intend to take any orders from the girl. With a snarl he made a leap for her face.

CHAPTER XV

A Puzzling Secret

NANCY might have been bitten if the postman had not acted quickly. As the girl dodged the angry animal, the man left the safety of the porch. He seized the whip from her hand and beat off the dog.

Nancy ran toward the cellar door. Cleverly she trapped the animal inside.

"That beast should be shot!" the mailman declared as he examined his torn trouser leg. "Are you the owner?"

"Indeed, I am not. He belongs to Mrs. Alexandra's grandson."

"The dog must be turned over to the authorities."

"I agree with you," Nancy nodded. "If he's allowed to stay here, someone may be bitten. I'll call the dog warden at once."

Anna, who had witnessed the scene from indoors, offered no objection when she learned of the decision. Rudy had caused her much annoyance, and his constant barking disturbed Mrs. Alexandra.

"Now that Madame Marie is so upset the dog should go," Anna said quietly.

Nancy called up the city pound, and presently a man arrived to take away the dangerous animal. Rudy resisted capture, and it finally became necessary to spray a sleeping fluid on him to subdue him. After the wagon pulled away, quiet descended upon the household.

"It is a great relief," sighed Anna, who now began to prepare a tray of food for her mistress.

A bell in the kitchen jingled.

"What is that?" Nancy inquired. "Not the door?"

"No," the servant explained. "It is Madame Marie summoning me. She has a silken bell cord beside her, which rings here in the kitchen and in my bedroom. Come, we will see what she wants."

Nancy followed Anna upstairs to a large room overlooking the garden. The walls were covered with silk hangings, the floor protected with an Oriental rug. A four-poster mahogany bed had figures of swans carved on the headboard. A canopy of blue velvet with fringe of gold hung above it.

"This is a queen's room indeed," thought Nancy.

Mrs. Alexandra, her face pale, tossed restlessly on a lace-covered pillow. Overnight she had seemed to age.

"Anna, why did you not come immediately?" Fretfully her mistress plucked at the ruby knob of the bell cord.

"I came as quickly as I could, Madame. There was a slight disturbance——"

"The dog?"

"Yes, but he will annoy you no more."

"I am so glad. His constant barking makes my head ache. It was good of Michael to send him away."

Nancy started to explain, but remained silent as the maid raised a finger to her lips.

"Anna, bring my clothing," Mrs. Alexandra ordered. "I cannot remain any longer in bed."

"But, Madame, after an attack it is important that you rest," the servant pleaded. "I will bring your dinner tray."

"I have no appetite."

"I'll sit beside you while you eat," offered Nancy, "and you can tell me stories of life at court."

She knew that the woman enjoyed company, and frequently forgot her troubles while talking of the past.

"In that case I will taste the food," Mrs. Alexandra murmured politely.

Nancy and Anna raised the old lady up in bed, bracing her with cushions. The maid then brought water in a silver basin. After washing her mistress's hands, she dried them on a towel of fine linen. The woman's initials and a royal crown were embroidered on it.

At first Mrs. Alexandra ate sparingly. But as Nancy encouraged her to talk of life at the palace, she seemed to forget her unhappiness. Soon she had finished the entire dinner.

"Madame Marie, would you not enjoy show-

ing Miss Nancy a few of your things?" Anna
wheedled, delighted that her mistress's spirits
were lifting. "The orchid silk sachet bags we
use to scent your clothing, for instance?"

"I should love to see them—everything!"
Nancy exclaimed.

At a nod from Mrs. Alexandra, Anna
brought one of the sweet-scented little bags and
laid it in the girl's hand. The cover of each one
was decorated with a hand-embroidered monogram.

"And here is one of Madame Marie's handkerchiefs," Anna said proudly. She offered
Nancy a dainty square of white batiste, embroidered in brown, with a lace border. "Note
the skillful mendings which were made by Madame herself."

"Even queens in my country are taught to
be thrifty," Mrs. Alexandra smiled. "Anna,
bring out the porcelain bowls from their hiding
place."

"But, Madame——"

"Nancy is our friend, Anna," the old lady
said irritably. "Your caution annoys me at
times. You keep everything hidden, because
you are afraid we shall be robbed. Why, you
even distrust my grandson!"

The servant bit her lip but made no reply.
Going to a carved mahogany chest, she unlocked
it with a huge brass key. One by one she removed porcelain bowls, enamel figurines, and a
number of treasures Nancy had seen before
downstairs.

"Do not forget The Footman!" Mrs. Alexandra ordered. "I wish to learn if Nancy can guess his secret."

Anna brought forth from the chest a lifelike figurine of porcelain. It stood about eight inches high and was unique, but not as attractive as some of Mrs. Alexandra's other treasures.

"This is my most prized possession," the woman declared gaily. "He looks like my own private footman at the palace. But also, he has a special significance. Nancy, can you guess what it is?"

The girl shook her head, waiting expectantly.

"The figurine represents one of the most courageous of the court servants. He helped me escape during the Revolution. When I fled, I took this little object with me."

"It isn't your jewel box, Mrs. Alexandra?"

"Yes. Is it not clever? I shall now reveal to you how it opens."

The woman reached for the little statue, but before she could show Nancy its secret, footsteps were heard on the staircase.

"Quick, Madame!" exclaimed Anna, startled.

With amazing speed she snatched The Footman from Mrs. Alexandra and hid it in the chest. She disposed of the other art treasures in similar fashion, and put the brass key under the rug.

"It is only Michael," Mrs. Alexandra said, recognizing her grandson's step.

"Nevertheless it is well that the treasures be kept out of sight," Anna insisted soberly.

Michael did not enter, but went on to his own room.

Not wanting to meet him, Nancy bade Mrs. Alexandra good-by. But she determined to come again soon to find out if The Footman were the jewel box to which the nightingale might refer.

As she was starting away from the house, Michael hurried down the walk after her. With flashing eyes, he confronted her.

"I heard you talking to my grandmother," he stormed. "What's the idea of coming here to make trouble?"

"Trouble?"

"First you left me stranded on Star Island——"

"That was none of my doing," Nancy replied coldly. "I will say, though, that you deserved it. Your conduct was certainly not like that of a prince."

"And then you deliberately got rid of my dog! One of the neighbors told me!"

"Your dog attacked the postman. Rudy's been sent away for ten days' observation."

"If Rudy bit anyone, you probably made him do it!"

"How ridiculous!"

"I've caught on that you're trying to turn everyone against me," Michael went on, "especially Grandmother."

"That isn't true."

"Let me tell you something!" The unpleasant man edged closer to Nancy. "If you come here again, you'll get more than you bargain for!"

"Is that a threat?"

"Call it what you like," the prince said insolently. "But remember—don't come here again."

Without waiting for the girl to reply, he reentered the house, slamming the door behind him.

"I'll come here as frequently as I wish!" Nancy thought angrily. "At least as long as Mrs. Alexandra wants me! He is the one who should be kept from the house. He isn't bringing his grandmother any happiness, and I'm afraid she already has given him more money than she can afford."

Sorely troubled, she walked toward home. For the first time in her life Nancy regretted that she had solved a mystery. By finding Prince Michael and restoring him to his grandmother, she feared she had only added to the gracious old lady's unhappiness.

CHAPTER XVI

The Fashion Parade

In RETURNING home, Nancy chose the familiar way, which led past Mr. Faber's shop. While still some distance from it, she noticed a man on the opposite side of the street, walking toward her with short, hurried steps. He resembled David Dorrance. As he drew closer she was certain it was he, but the man, though glancing at her, passed with no sign of recognition.

"That must be Dorrance's double—the pickpocket!" Nancy thought excitedly. "This time I'll catch him!"

Turning, she crossed the street, and followed the man. Not once did he look back, nor did he pause, until he reached the revolving doors of an office building.

Nancy quickened her pace, fearing that she might lose sight of him. At that moment he halted deliberately, keeping his face slightly averted. Half turning toward the girl, he waved a white handkerchief.

"Wrong again!" Nancy thought in disgust, stopping short. "Will I never learn to recognize that fellow?"

Recovering from the unpleasant surprise, she called Mr. Dorrance's name. Instead of replying, he entered the revolving doors and was lost to view.

Disappointed, Nancy retraced her way down the street. She had gone but fifty feet when she saw old Mr. Faber running in her direction. The shop owner's coat was awry, and his long gray hair blew wildly in the wind.

"I've been robbed!" he shouted to those on the street. "The thief went this way! Did anyone see him?"

Recognizing Nancy, the antique dealer paused to get his breath. He was so excited that he was difficult to understand, but she gathered that a very few minutes before a valuable gold and enamel penknife had disappeared from his show counter.

"It was a genuine eighteenth century piece," the old man cried. "Never can I replace it."

"How was it taken?" Nancy asked quickly.

"Several customers were in my shop. A short fellow asked to see the penknife. He took so long to decide I waited on the others."

"And the man and the knife disappeared?"

"Yes! Did a short fellow come this way?"

"I saw one enter the Monroe Building," Nancy revealed. "But I'm sure he's not the one who stole the knife!" she added, frowning thoughtfully.

A few people had gathered about, but no one had a clue to the thief.

"It is hopeless then to recover my property," Mr. Faber said despairingly. "I may as well return— Oh, over there!" he cried suddenly, pointing to a man in a brown suit who had come from a store across the street. "There he is now! The one who took the pen-knife!"

The person Faber pointed out was a little way down the block beyond the antique shop. He resembled David Dorrance very closely. This time Nancy had no doubt that he was the long-sought pickpocket. Dorrance was some distance away in the Monroe Building.

"Mr. Faber, you telephone to the police!" Nancy advised. "I'll trail the thief!"

"Hurry, hurry," the old shop owner pleaded.

The girl tried desperately to cross the street, but traffic was heavy. She found herself stranded in a center safety zone. The man identified by Faber was still in sight, but before she could reach him, he leaped into an empty taxi.

"Wait!" Nancy shouted to the driver.

The chauffeur did not hear her, but his passenger turned his head. Seeing the girl, he took a handkerchief from his pocket, and very deliberately waved it! Then the cab sped on, presently turning a corner.

Nancy stood still, completely bewildered. "How could Dorrance have gotten here from the Monroe Building so quickly?" she asked herself. "He must have wings!"

Many thoughts raced through her mind as

she recrossed the street to Faber's shop. The more she mulled over the matter, the more she became convinced that Dorrance could not possibly have gone from one place to the other in such a short time.

"They were two different people!" she concluded. "But they both waved handkerchiefs!"

Had the thief learned the method of identification the other used when seeing Nancy?

"That first man didn't give me the signal right away," she reflected. "So the second one must have been Dorrance."

Before she had a chance to reflect further, a police car rushed up to Faber's shop. The little man was so upset he was glad to have the girl tell the story. She started it by advising the two officers to go with her at once to the Monroe Building.

"We may not be too late to nab the pickpocket, if a hunch of mine is correct," she said

They rushed down the street, and the men searched the place. No one resembling the suspect was there. Discouraged, the three returned to the antique shop, where Faber described the stolen penknife.

"It was set with pearls, and is a rare piece," he concluded.

"We'll do what we can to locate it," one of the policemen promised. "That pickpocket is a slippery fellow. We've had that apartment house at Main and Water watched constantly, but no one resembling the thief has turned up yet.''

''The pickpocket is too smart to show up there again,'' said the other officer.

Nancy already had concluded the thief was very smart. After the police had driven away, her recent thoughts about Dorrance and his double came back to her. On the spur of the moment she asked a startling question.

''Mr. Faber, can you describe the man who bought the pistol which used to hang on the wall here?''

The dealer scratched his head. ''It is hard to remember. I have so many people looking who do not buy. Why do you ask?''

''A man tried to sell my father an old revolver,'' she replied. ''It looked very much like the one that used to hang here. This person happens to resemble a pickpocket, who may be the person that took the penknife.''

''I see,'' reflected Faber, looking into space. Suddenly he tapped his forehead and smiled. ''Now I remember. The man who bought it did look very much like my customer this afternoon. But there is one big difference.''

''What is that?'' asked Nancy eagerly.

''Their hands. I do not pay so much attention to the face as to the hands,'' explained Faber. ''Sometimes I forget a face, but never a hand. I learned from my skillful father how a person's character may be deduced from nervous fingers or a tight grasp.''

"That's a very interesting observation," said his listener. "You have given me something to work on."

On the way home Nancy reflected upon the important clue Mr. Faber had given her. When she reached the house, however, her thoughts were turned toward other things.

"Tomorrow is the first day of the Fashion Show," Hannah reminded her. "This afternoon you must shampoo your hair, and attend to other things for the performance."

The following morning Nancy attended a final rehearsal. Early that afternoon she presented herself at the dressing room of the Woman's Club for the first performance. Katherine, pale and nervous, arrived a few minutes later, accompanied by Helen Corning.

"Did you bring the hair ornament?" Nancy asked anxiously.

"Safe and sound," laughed Helen, producing the ruby and diamond piece. "And Katherine pressed the gown at the last second. That was what delayed us."

"Is it time to dress yet?"

"I think you should," Helen urged. "The audience is arriving early, so the show will start exactly on the minute."

With painstaking care, Nancy put on the blue flowered gown. The skirt swung gracefully to the floor. Katherine pinned up the train, so that it would not collect dust from the carpet.

"If I forget to take the pins out before the show starts, all is lost!" the young designer murmured nervously.

"How do I look?" Nancy inquired, preening herself before a full-length mirror.

"Like the prettiest picture in a fashion book!" Helen praised her lavishly. "Oh, I hope for Katherine's sake you win the grand prize!" she added in a whisper.

Soon the dressing room was crowded with excited, chattering models. Everyone praised Nancy's costume, and many of the girls gazed at it with envy.

A few minutes before the show was scheduled to start, Bess and George came backstage to view their chum in all her splendor.

"Nearly everyone of importance in River Heights is here," they told her. "Even the Mayor! And plenty of photographers, reporters, and artists!"

"Mrs. Alexandra came too, with Anna," Bess went on. "You should have seen heads turn when she walked in! She is so regal looking."

"She made the effort for Katherine's sake," Nancy replied. "How kind of her!"

"She do it for you, not for me," Katherine denied quickly. "Mrs. Alexandra like you very much, Nancy."

"And I like her, too," the other responded warmly. "I am glad she is feeling well enough to be here."

The orchestra had begun to play, and the models were told to take their places. Those wearing street clothes came first, then the afternoon dresses, and finally the evening gowns. Nervously Katherine unpinned Nancy's train and adjusted the headdress.

"Now!" she whispered, her voice tense.

The moment had arrived for her model to walk out upon the stage!

Nancy made an effective entrance, carrying herself well. She slowly rotated, so that the audience might see the Renaissance gown to advantage. Each model had been greeted with a polite ripple of applause. Now the handclapping was loud and spontaneous.

Gracefully Nancy approached the carpeted steps which would carry her to the level of the audience. She saw Mrs. Alexandra's beaming face, and directly below her in the front row, Mr. Ellington, the artist. To her secret delight he nodded approvingly, and began to sketch.

"He likes the gown!" she thought joyously.

Keeping perfect time to the music, Nancy moved down the first two steps. She felt at ease now, confident that she was making a favorable impression.

As she reached the third step, there was a sudden sideways movement of the board beneath the carpet. Frantically Nancy tried to keep her balance.

Instead she plunged headlong toward the floor!

CHAPTER XVII

WANTED—A CLUE

As NANCY pitched forward on the steps at the crowded Fashion Show, Mr. Ellington, the artist, jumped up. The girl fell directly into the young man's arms.

"Oh!" she murmured, exceedingly embarrassed.

There had been an audible gasp from the audience, and the music had ceased abruptly. For a moment many had feared the girl would be injured.

The accident had been caused by a loose board, which a careless carpenter had failed to nail down. Covered by carpet, it had shifted beneath the weight of the various models. When Nancy had reached the step it had given way entirely.

"Are you hurt?" Mr. Ellington asked, as he assisted her to regain her balance.

Nancy shook her head, trying desperately to recover her poise. She felt sick at heart, not so much for herself as for Katherine. Any chance of her winning a prize was gone, she felt sure.

"Don't let this disturb you," the artist whispered kindly. "It wasn't your fault! The judges can't blame you!"

Thus encouraged, Nancy smiled bravely. The orchestra began to play again. She glided down the center aisle and back, disappearing at last by a side door into the stage wings.

The other models who followed her in the style parade did not descend the stairway. As soon as the performance ended, carpenters were sent to repair the faulty step.

"Oh, Katherine, I knew I would ruin your chances!" Nancy cried when she met the designer. "Why did I have to stumble?"

"It wasn't your fault," Helen Corning said loyally before the other girl could reply.

"No, indeed," echoed Katherine. "Tomorrow you make a grand entrance!"

"I hope so," Nancy sighed. "I'll have to do something to atone for today."

Although everyone declared that the accident had been unavoidable, the three girls did not feel very cheerful. They brightened, however, when Mr. Ellington sought out Katherine to tell her that he considered her design the most original one entered in the show.

"If I were one of the judges, I'd vote to give you first prize," he declared warmly.

Katherine blushed and became confused. He talked for a long while, causing Nancy to think his interest more than a professional one.

"What a grand couple they would make!" she remarked to Helen. "They have so much in common."

"Mr. Ellington is very charming," Helen agreed. "Isn't it a pity Michael couldn't have a little of his polish?"

"Sh!" Nancy warned suddenly.

Mrs. Alexandra was approaching, followed by Anna. If the grandmother had heard the remark, she gave no indication of it. She was profuse in her praise of Katherine's work, and the way in which Nancy had modeled the dress.

"Both of you girls are talented," she declared, smiling. "Oh, I do not mean it takes talent to show off a gown well," she went on as Nancy started to protest. "I mean your ability as a detective."

"Some day you must have Nancy tell you about the cases she has solved," Helen said enthusiastically. "However, she is so modest, she probably won't do it!" she added with a teasing grin.

"Perhaps I can hear about them tomorrow," replied Mrs. Alexandra, a twinkle in her eye. "Nancy, will you have luncheon with me at one o'clock? As you say in America," she smiled delightfully, "we have some unfinished business to which we should attend."

"Thank you, I'm afraid I can't come this time. I am due here before three for the afternoon performance."

"I shall see that you are not late."

Still Nancy hesitated to accept the invitation. Her last meeting with Michael had been most unpleasant, and she feared he might create a scene should he find her a guest in his home.

"Michael will not be there," Anna whispered
as if reading the girl's thoughts.

"I'll be delighted to come, Mrs. Alexandra,"
Nancy accepted at once.

After the former queen mother and her companion had gone, Michael again became the
topic of conversation. Katherine, who rejoined the girls, admitted to her friends that
the young man had called several times at her
shop.

"He annoy me with attentions I do not like!
He send me flowers! He ask me for dates! Always I say 'No,' but it does no good."

"Michael is a pest in every way," Helen declared.

"I'd give anything if I never had traced him
for Mrs. Alexandra," Nancy said soberly.

"I don't see how she can put up with him,"
Helen added.

When Nancy appeared at the woman's home
the next day, the topic of Michael was studi-
ously avoided. A delicious luncheon was
served during which biscuits were passed in a
quaint wooden basket with a royal crown on the
handle. As the hostess noticed her guest looking at it with particular interest, she remarked:

"In the happy days before the Revolution I
used to go on long tramps and gather mush-
rooms in that basket. It was a delightful
pastime."

At the close of the meal Mrs. Alexandra
asked Anna to bring The Footman jewel box to
her. Almost tenderly, the former queen held

the quaint porcelain and enamel figure in her hands.

"I shall now open it for you," she said to Nancy. "Can you guess how it is done?"

"By a secret spring?"

"Yes, first I press the little fellow here."

Mrs. Alexandra's exploring fingers touched The Footman's left hand. To the girl's amazement, the black coat of the figure loosened, enabling the elderly lady to remove it. She pressed another spring, and a panel at the back of the case slid open. Inside were a ruby ring, an unset emerald, a necklace of matched pearls, and two diamond bracelets.

"All that remain of my jewels," Mrs. Alexandra said, her voice trembling with emotion. "Piece by piece I sold the others."

"These are exquisite," Nancy replied. After a moment she asked, "Did the box ever contain anything except jewelry?"

"No, it has always been used for that purpose. You are disappointed, perhaps?"

Nancy hastened to correct such an impression. "I am not disappointed, Mrs. Alexandra. I'll admit, though, that the little nightingale's words led me to believe this box might contain something else of importance."

"Have you also thought out what it might be, my pretty detective?"

"Katherine has told me the people of your country have many secrets," the girl replied. "One of them is a process for making uncrackable enamel. I admit I wondered if The Footman might be hiding the lost formula."

Mrs. Alexandra tried to suppress a smile. "My dear," she said kindly, "I wonder if you have not misinterpreted the song of the nightingale? To me its words are too indistinct to be taken seriously."

"Perhaps, but we know the song was added long after the Easter egg was made," Nancy reminded her.

"Until Mr. Faber told you differently, I assumed that the nightingale was exactly as it had been created for me."

"You have no idea when the addition was made?"

"It must have been during the early days of the Revolution, for that is the only time the gift was out of my hands. I was away from the palace when the trouble started. There was such turmoil that I could not get back for some time."

The woman stopped speaking, and tears gathered in her eyes. Nancy tried to direct the woman's sad thoughts about the loss of the royal family into another channel.

"When you returned, was the Easter egg in a different place from where it usually was kept?" she asked.

"Now that I think back, it was."

"The song may have been added while you were away," Nancy suggested. "Perhaps someone tried to provide you with an important clue—a clue meant for no other person."

"I never gave it serious thought until now."

"Who besides yourself had access to the Easter egg, Mrs. Alexandra?"

"Only a few trusted servants in the palace."

"Who in your country was skillful at making music boxes?" Nancy asked eagerly.

"Old Conrad Nicholas," Mrs. Alexandra replied without hesitation.

"Who was he?"

"The husband of Nada's sister. Nada was the nurse of my grandson Michael."

"Would she have been able to get the Easter egg?"

"Yes."

"Why, it all fits in beautifully!" Nancy exclaimed, elated. "Mrs. Alexandra, I'm convinced some jewel box contains a vital clue, and it must be this Footman. Perhaps it holds a secret of greater value than all your jewels!"

"But what could it be?"

Without attempting to answer the question, Nancy went on, "The box may have another opening. The legs of The Footman have not been used to store gems in."

"That's true," Mrs. Alexandra returned.

"Let's search there," Nancy urged eagerly.

"My dear, I already have examined the little statue from his head to the tip of his boots! The secret, if there is one, has been cleverly hidden."

"Mrs. Alexandra, do you mind if I try?"

"By all means see what you can find!"

Smiling, the former queen placed the jewel box in the girl's hands. With trembling fingers, Nancy began to explore the porcelain and enamel figure inch by inch.

CHAPTER XVIII

A Question of Honesty

ALTHOUGH Nancy twisted and turned the little Footman, tapping the figurine here and there, she could find no additional spring or mechanism. The only opening appeared to be the one with which she already was familiar.

"You see, my dear, there is no clue in the jewel box," said Mrs. Alexandra at last.

"I can't find it, at least." Sighing, Nancy returned the figurine to her hostess. "Some day, with your permission, I may try again."

"By all means. You have awakened my interest, too."

"I can't allow a little nightingale to outwit me!" the girl said with a determined smile.

A clock chimed the hour of two-thirty. Reminded that she would be late for the Fashion Show unless she should leave at once, Nancy hurried away.

A few minutes later, upon reaching the Woman's Club, she was surprised to see an excited crowd near the main entrance. A policeman had placed someone under arrest.

Approaching closer, the girl observed that this person, who was arguing loudly with the officer, closely resembled David Dorrance. At

141

the same instant, the man turned and recognized her.

"Miss Drew, tell this policeman he's made a
mistake!" he pleaded.

"I'm not sure—" she began, but he cut her
off.

"Sure, you recognize me! See!"

He gave the familiar white handkerchief
signal. Nancy had but a moment to spare, for
she was late now. She did not know what to do.
As she hesitated, Dorrance added:

"I came here to see the show. I read in the
paper that you were to be in it, so I wanted to
see you."

As he spoke, Nancy became convinced that he
was the man who had come to her home. She
took a long look at his hands. How she wished
she could tell him and the real pickpocket apart
by this method!

"I believe this man may not be the person
you want," she said to the officer. "At least,
he's not the one who stole the wallet of a man
named Baum."

The policeman knew Nancy. In an aside he
asked her if she thought he should let the man
go. The girl hesitated to decide, for she had
not forgotten the double handkerchief episode
on Main Street. Finally she told the officer she
certainly could not identify Dorrance as the
wanted pickpocket.

"Go on in, then," he told the man. "Sorry
to have made the mistake."

Dorrance would have lingered to chat with

Nancy, but she had no time for him. Hastening to the dressing room, she quickly donned the Renaissance gown, just as the orchestra began to play.

"I'll try to do better than yesterday," she promised Katherine, when it was her turn to enter the stage. "I hope I haven't spoiled your chance for a prize."

With perfect composure and a grace not to be matched by the other models, Nancy went through her simple routine. No accident marred the performance. She returned to the wings amid thunderous applause.

"You were a sensation!" Helen praised her warmly. "Listen to that clapping!"

"Ned and his friends are out there. I guess that accounts for some of it," Nancy laughed.

"Nonsense," Helen retorted gaily. "Even Ned couldn't make that much noise! You and that gorgeous gown are the talk of the show!"

During a brief intermission, Nancy wandered out into the audience. Before she got all the way down the center aisle, which was crowded with people walking around, a woman close by uttered a piercing wail.

"My pocketbook! It has been stolen!"

Immediately the entire room was thrown into confusion. In the resulting excitement, Nancy spied David Dorrance slipping out the exit.

"Now maybe he can explain a thing or two!" she thought grimly. "I'm going to settle this double business once and for all!"

Forgetting her part in the show, Nancy sped

after the fleeing man. When she reached the door, she saw him hurrying toward an alley.

"Wait!" she called.

The man turned, but did not pause. Nancy spied two little boys directly ahead, and shouted to them:

"Stop that fellow! Don't let him get away!"

The lads attempted to block the man's path, but he shoved them away angrily. Nancy ran after him as fast as she could. The long evening gown impeded her progress. Unnoticed, the silk train dragged in the dust.

Despite the handicap of her clothing, the girl began to gain on the thief, but at the end of the alley, the man darted around a corner. There he saw a long strand of barbed wire lying on the ground. Seizing it, he threw it in such a way that Nancy could not fail to run against the sharp barbs.

Unsuspecting, she ran around the corner, straight into the wire. Her gown caught in a dozen places, tearing badly. It caused her to halt.

"Guess that will hold her for a few minutes!" chuckled the man ahead, disappearing once more.

Nancy sought frantically to free herself. By the time she had loosened the dress, pursuit was useless.

"Oh, this beautiful gown!" the girl thought sadly, as she saw that it had been torn beyond repair. "What will Katherine say? I've ruined her chances completely now!"

Out of breath and disheveled, the girl returned to the clubhouse. It was time for the second half of the Fashion Show to begin, and spectators were returning from the lobby to their seats.

Suddenly in the throng Nancy saw David Dorrance!

"Why, Miss Drew, what has happened to you?" he asked, walking over to her.

The man was perfectly composed. There was no indication, either in his breathing or the color of his face, that he had been running.

"I mistook him again for the pickpocket!" Nancy thought, chagrined.

To him she replied that she had had a little accident. Quickly the girl sought a side door to escape the crowd. She did not want anyone else to notice her torn gown.

"It is very strange that Dorrance and the thief are so often in the same place," she thought. "I think it's too much of a coincidence. As soon as I change my clothes, I'm going to talk to the police about it!"

Nancy found Katherine and Helen waiting for her in the dressing room. When they saw the ruined evening gown, they were distressed.

"Oh, Nancy, how did it happen?" Helen managed to say at last.

Making no attempt to excuse herself, she told how she had pursued the pickpocket.

"I ought to stick to sleuthing and give up trying to model in fashion shows," she concluded grimly. "The two certainly don't mix."

"What are we to do?" Helen asked, sinking into a chair. "The dress can't be mended."

"I shan't appear in the show again until tomorrow afternoon. That gives us twenty-four hours. Couldn't you duplicate the dress, Katherine? You had a good bit of material left over."

"In so short a time? It would be impossible."

"Maybe part of it could be saved," said Nancy, noticing that Katherine was on the verge of tears. "The sleeves are in perfect condition."

"And so is all the back except the train," Helen encouraged her, taking new hope. "Couldn't you just make a new front and replace the train?"

"I'll help you, Katherine," Nancy offered. "I could sew all night, if necessary."

The designer made a hasty examination of the gown. A minute later her eyes lighted up. "I can do it!" she decided suddenly. "Undress quickly, Nancy. No moment must we lose."

Without waiting to see the remainder of the Fashion Show, the girls hastened to Katherine's shop. For two hours they sewed steadily. By then it was evident that the work could be finished on time.

"We go home now and rest," Katherine urged. "I finish the dress by noonday tomorrow."

The attractive young designer locked the

door of her shop, and the three girls walked down the street together. At the corner Nancy left the others to go to the police station. There she reported her suspicions regarding Dorrance and his double.

"It seems strange to me that those two men should always be in the same place at the same time," she said to the chief.

The officer gave her a friendly smile. "Do you think they are twins?" he asked.

"They look enough alike," Nancy replied. "At first I thought only one was dishonest; that probably his brother knew this, and was trying to protect him."

"That still may be true."

"Now I'm wondering," Nancy continued, "whether the other one is as innocent of the thefts as he seems to be."

"I'm glad you've told me this," said the chief. "The truth is, my men haven't got to first base in catching that pickpocket, or solving the mystery of all the thefts going on in River Heights. You've given us a new clue to work on."

He called together several policemen in the room and told them Nancy's theory. He ended by asking if they were going to let Miss Drew outwit them in nabbing the guilty persons. Several of the officers saw the twinkle in their superior's eye and smiled, but two of the younger patrolmen looked uneasy.

"I guess those two younger men were pretty annoyed with me!" Nancy thought as she left the police station. "Afraid I'll take some glory from them!"

She went on home, looking forward to a quiet evening, as she wanted to think out several angles of her other mystery, the Clue in the Jewel Box. Upon arriving at the house, she found an urgent note awaiting her from Mrs. Alexandra's servant Anna. It requested the girl to come to the woman's house as soon as possible.

"Of course I'll go," Nancy decided, "but I'll hate to meet Michael. He certainly told me in no uncertain terms to stay away from there!"

Nancy thought it best to go to the back entrance. Anna met her at the door, and they conversed in the kitchen. To Nancy's question about where the prince was, the woman replied that he was not at home.

"Is Mrs. Alexandra ill?" the girl inquired anxiously. "Your note——"

"She is sick here." Anna indicated the region of her heart. "Sick because of Michael. Oh, that boy!"

"What has he done now, Anna?"

"I learned something dreadful only yesterday. She has given him many valuable articles to sell."

"I knew Mrs. Alexandra had sent him once to Mr. Faber."

"Not once, but many times. And he has gone to other shops. The prices paid have not been high. Much too low for what the things are worth."

"How dreadful!" said Nancy.

"Something is very much wrong," Anna declared, her eyes flashing. "I say it is time to ask questions of Michael. But Madame Marie will not do it!"

"Doesn't he bring back signed receipts?"

"He gives her nothing, except a few dollars. When I try to ask him questions, he tells me to mind my business; that I am only a servant."

Nancy's mind was working fast. She decided on a bold step.

"Anna, can you give me a list of the pieces Mrs. Alexandra has sold through Michael?" she requested. "Also the amounts which he paid her?"

"I have it all here," the woman declared, whisking a paper from the pocket of her apron.

"I'll check the items at once with the shopkeepers," Nancy promised. "In the meantime, don't tell Mrs. Alexandra, for it would only distress her."

A door slammed and Michael's whistle was heard in the hall.

"I must go quickly before he sees me," the girl whispered, opening the screen door.

She slipped through the garden to the back street, and went at once to Mr. Faber's shop. The antique dealer was looking out the front door as Nancy arrived.

"Oh, Mr. Faber," she greeted him, "may I talk with you a moment?"

"Certainly," he replied, noting her agitation. "Is anything wrong?"

"I don't know," Nancy replied, deciding to come straight to the point. "Are you willing to tell me how much you paid Michael for the ring he sold to you?"

"Three hundred dollars It would have brought more if he had been willing to wait for me to find a buyer. He insisted Mrs. Alexandra have cash at once."

Nancy inspected the sales list she had brought with her. According to Anna's notation, Michael had given his grandmother only one hundred dollars for the ring. Apparently he had kept the remaining sum for himself.

"Mr. Faber, I am sorry to say this, but I think Michael is dishonest," she said quietly. "Please examine this list."

The antique dealer frowned as he read the amounts paid by various shopkeepers for other treasures.

"These are worth far more than this paper indicates Mrs. Alexandra received," he declared. "Come into the shop while I telephone."

His anger aroused, Mr. Faber called one of the firms listed. He learned that a jade and enamel vase had been sold for a large amount, but only a small percentage of the money received had been turned over to the owner. Another dealer reported he had given the young man five hundred dollars for an antique tapestry. Yet only ninety-five dollars of this had been turned over to Mrs. Alexandra!

"Michael has cheated his grandmother!"

Mr. Faber exclaimed. "Oh, how could a prince from my native land be so cruel!"

"It's just possible Mrs. Alexandra intended Michael to have the rest as spending money, but did not wish to tell Anna this," Nancy suggested, as the old man became extremely excited.

"It will kill Madame Alexandra to learn that her grandson is a common thief," Mr. Faber declared, paying no attention.

"We must do nothing until we are sure," said Nancy with determination.

"This is the saddest day of my life," Mr. Faber said brokenly. "To think that Prince Michael would resort to such practice!"

It was dark when Nancy finally left the antique shop. But dinner was to be late, so she decided to walk home rather than wait for a bus. She reached her own street and finally turned in at the Drew residence. The windows of the house were dark.

"Hannah must be in the kitchen, and probably has forgotten to turn on the front lights," the girl thought.

Suddenly, from behind the tall bushes framing the porch, arose two men. To prevent recognition they had pulled their hats low, and each held a hand across his face.

"All right!" muttered one of them in signal to his companion.

Nancy started to scream, but a hand was clapped over her mouth, and she was held in a grip of steel.

CHAPTER XIX

A THREAT

As NANCY struggled vainly to free herself,
one of the men spoke. His voice plainly was
disguised.

"Miss Drew, I'm warning you that if you
don't do as we tell you, you'll be sorry, and
your father sorrier. You've got to mind your
own business!"

Nancy squirmed sideways, trying to see her
captors. Their hats were pulled so low and
they kept their faces so well covered, it was impossible to see their features.

"How about it?" the taller of the two de
manded, giving her a rough shake. "Will you
promise?"

"Promise what?" Nancy mumbled, as the
hand on her mouth was lifted slightly.

"Stop trying to be a detective!"

"Are you afraid I'll have you arrested?"
Nancy countered.

"Come on, quit the stalling!" the man said
angrily. "Either promise, or take the conse-
quences."

An automobile was coming down the street,
its headlights cutting a path along the dark

pavement. The engine had a familiar sound, and Nancy took new heart. She must keep on sparring for time!

"No, I'll not promise anything," she answered boldly, struggling to break free. "Take your hands off me!"

The car, which had been approaching slowly, turned into the Drew driveway. Nancy gave a quick jerk, freeing her mouth for a second.

"Help! Help!" she shouted.

The man who held her gave the girl a sudden push which sent her reeling into the porch rail.

"Come on!" he snapped to his companion. "We'd better get out of here!"

Still keeping their faces covered, the two men jumped off the porch. Crouching low, they ran along the hedge, and disappeared into the protecting shadows of the garden next door.

Carson Drew leaped from his automobile and hurried to Nancy's side. She had recovered her balance and come down the steps.

"Why did you scream?" he demanded anxiously. "What happened?"

"Follow me! Two men——"

Breathlessly Nancy told him how his timely arrival had saved her. She and Mr. Drew quickly ran in the direction the men had taken and searched around the garden, but the strangers had disappeared.

"Did you recognize either of them, Nancy?"

"No, they took care to disguise their voices. Possibly they were Michael and a friend."

"How were they dressed?"

"It was too dark for me to see them. One of the men was rather short—in fact, his build resembled that of David Dorrance's double."

"He's afraid you're getting too hot on his trail," Mr. Drew said thoughtfully.

Nancy told of her suspicions and of her report to the police.

"I'm glad you told them," he replied. "And hereafter, let them run after the pickpocket. If the threat tonight was from the thief and his pals, your trailing him is getting to a point of danger. Next time I might not be around to save you!" he added affectionately.

"I've been hoping to recover the money for the Boys Club and the papers stolen from you," his daughter replied.

"The money is probably spent by this time," Mr. Drew guessed. "Don't worry any more about my wallet. Buy me another for my birthday!"

He put away the automobile which had been left in the driveway. Nancy helped him lock the double doors of the garage, and they went into the house together. As they sat at dinner a little later, she observed that her father looked worried.

"Nancy," he said quietly, "I wish you would stop taking so much interest in Mrs. Alexandra's affairs."

"Why, Dad!" Nancy stared at her father in dismay. "I can't abandon the dear old lady to Michael's clutches. Why, only today I learned that he has been robbing her of rather large sums of money. Just look at this paper!'' she added, getting the slip from her purse.

Mr. Drew inspected the sales notations obtained through Anna and Mr. Faber.

"You don't expect Mrs. Alexandra to believe that her grandson is a thief?'' he inquired as he returned the paper.

"No, and I don't intend to tell her until I have proved my facts.''

"Don't do anything until I've had time to consider the legal angle,'' her father advised. "I'll think over the matter, so we'll know exactly what's what before you talk to Mrs. Alexandra.''

"I'll be very glad to wait,'' Nancy responded. "Telling the poor woman the truth will probably end our friendship, anyway.''

"You're sure that even after the threat tonight you want to continue work on the case?'' her father asked.

"It does add up to that. Why, maybe those men who stopped me tonight aren't bad at all!'' Nancy grinned impishly.

"No?''

"They could have been disgruntled policemen who are afraid I'm too active as a detective. Two of the younger ones at the police station looked rather annoyed at me when the chief asked me to help him.''

"Now that is a theory,'' Mr. Drew replied, amused by his daughter's efforts to win her point. "At least promise me you'll not try to track down any pickpockets by yourself.''

"I'll call in Assistants Bess and George," Nancy laughed. "By the way, Dad, what is the latest news concerning the Boys Club? I haven't heard you speak of it in days."

"That's because there is nothing encouraging to report," Mr. Drew responded drearily.

"Will the boys lose their club building?"

"I am afraid so, Nancy. The heirs say they are not interested in the street urchins of River Heights. They propose to rent the place to a business concern."

"Can't you get out an injunction or something?"

"Not in this case," Mr. Drew smiled. "The heirs are within their rights. If only I were a wealthy man, I would provide those newsboys and their friends with a fine clubhouse and a farm they could use as a summer camp."

The telephone rang. Mrs. Gruen answered it, and then reported that the call was for Nancy.

"I think it is Helen Corning," the housekeeper reported. "At least the voice was much like hers."

Fearing that there might be some new difficulty regarding the torn Fashion Show gown, Nancy ran to talk to her friend.

"For once I haven't a scrap of bad news to report," Helen assured her. "Mr. Ellington called up and wants us to organize a straw ride. Of course he will be Katherine's partner."

"Tonight?"

"No, tomorrow after the evening performance. He suggests we go to the Red Lion Inn for supper and dancing."

"A straw ride would be fun!" Nancy approved instantly. "Tell me more about it."

"Mr. Ellington is sure Katherine is going to win the grand prize at the Fashion Show, so he wants to entertain for her. Unfortunately he has to work out of town, so he'll not join us until we reach the Inn," Helen explained.

For some time the girls discussed plans for the straw ride, working out every detail. A window not far from where Nancy sat was open, and the curtains fluttered in the breeze. Once they moved far enough for anyone looking in that direction to have seen a man crouching outside, listening to the telephone conversation. Nancy had her back turned, and did not notice.

"We'll have a grand time tomorrow night," she declared before hanging up the receiver. "Especially if Katherine wins the big prize!"

Wishing to appear fresh for the next day's Fashion Show, Nancy went to bed early. Sleep refused to come. For a long while she tossed on her pillow, thinking of one mystery after another which confronted her. Of them all, she was particularly intrigued over the nightingale's words, "Clue in Jewel Box."

"The jewel box *must* be The Footman," she thought over and over. "The queen mother's family and trusted servants knew it was the one holding her most valuable pieces."

Nancy felt that if the secret could be revealed, something of such importance to Mrs. Alexandra might be uncovered that it would make up for the dishonesty and unattractiveness of the prince.

"That little Footman must have a second aperture," she reflected.

Try as she would, Nancy could think of no method, previously overlooked, for opening it. Nor did morning bring any solution to the vexing problem.

The matter continued to plague her throughout the day, even occupying her thoughts as she went through her afternoon routine at the Fashion Show. Then, just as she left the building, an idea flashed into the girl's mind.

"That may be it!" she thought excitedly. "I must go to Mrs. Alexandra's home at once. I only hope that I'll not find Michael there!"

CHAPTER XX

The Prize Winner

BLINDS were drawn at the Alexandra home, but Anna opened the door almost as soon as Nancy rang the bell. The servant explained that she had softened the light for her ailing mistress.

"Madame is very low in spirit." Anna dropped her voice discreetly. "It is Michael! This morning he asked her to give him a very valuable bracelet to sell."

"She didn't do it?"

"Not yet, but she is considering it very seriously. Oh, Miss Drew, can you not do something to save what remains of my good lady's fortune?"

"I hope to, Anna. I have proof that Michael robbed his grandmother of various sums of money."

"She will never believe it."

"I'm afraid not," Nancy sighed. "And anyway, there's a legal angle. Being related, he could say she gave it to him. My father is going to see about that. But I came here for another reason. Michael isn't at home, is he?"

"Yes, he is," Anna admitted, scowling. "He is with his grandmother now."

"Then I will leave and come another time."

159

"No, wait," the woman urged. "Hide in this closet. I will send Michael out."

Nancy secreted herself in the hall closet as instructed. She did not have long to wait. Soon she heard the young man arguing loudly with Anna.

"You always want me to go on errands for you!" he complained. "I'm a prince and you're supposed to wait on me."

An outside door slammed and Nancy knew that the grandson had gone. A moment later Anna came to release her.

"I have announced to Madame that you are here," she told Nancy. "She will see you at once in her bedroom."

No time was to be lost, for Michael might return at any moment. Accordingly, Nancy did not waste words as she explained to Mrs. Alexandra why she had come.

"Do you mind if I try once more to open the Footman jewel box?" she requested earnestly. "I have an idea which I think may work."

Mrs. Alexandra smiled, but bade Anna bring the precious little statue. As Nancy took it, she said:

"When I was a little girl my grandmother gave me a very old music box which had belonged to her. It had a secret drawer in it, which opened in a peculiar fashion. I'm going to try that method now."

The girl's fingers explored the figurine. "If only it will work——"

With increasing interest Mrs. Alexandra

watched Nancy skillfully manipulate the jewel box. Suddenly the queen mother gave a cry of delight.

"My Footman's boot! It is coming off!"

Nancy nodded, and drew a quick breath. Her theory had been correct!

"But there is no opening in the foot," Mrs. Alexandra added, disappointed.

Nancy peeked into the tiny boot. Thrusting her little finger into it, she loosened a folded piece of paper.

"This must be the clue that the little nightingale tried to tell us!" she exclaimed, drawing out the small sheet.

Nancy longed to look at the paper, but instead, politely offered it to her hostess. Mrs. Alexandra adjusted her glasses, and pondered a long time over the words scrawled on the paper. Nancy began to doubt that she ever would reveal the contents.

"Anna," the woman requested at last, "please leave us alone for a few minutes."

As soon as the servant had withdrawn, the former queen offered Nancy the paper. The girl was unable to read the words, for they were in a foreign language. Mrs. Alexandra, her voice vibrant with excitement, translated them in a whisper.

"This information is amazing!" the girl replied. "You probably——"

"Sh!" the woman warned. "Do not speak aloud of this great secret. No one must know of it yet—not even Anna."

"Neither you nor I can carry out the instructions on this paper," said Nancy, "so we must tell someone."

"You must ask your father to help you, or perhaps that fine young man I see so often with you," advised Mrs. Alexandra.

"Ned?" Nancy asked, flushing.

"Yes, he seems to be very capable."

"Oh, he is, Mrs. Alexandra! And he's just the person to help me. I'd ask my father, but he's out of town."

"Then choose Ned as your helper if you wish," the elderly lady said slowly. "The task is one which must be done. After this is over, I shall know how to proceed. Uncertainty is hard to bear."

From the window Nancy saw Michael coming back with a package.

"I must go now," she said hurriedly. "I'll report to you as soon as I can."

Anna had met the young man on the front walk, and engaged him in conversation until Nancy could leave by the rear door. He was talking in loud tones which carried to the girl.

"I'm too busy to be running to the store for you," he said crossly. "And you don't need all this stuff, anyway. I won't be here to dinner tonight, and maybe not all night, either!"

After leaving the house, Nancy returned to her own home in a state of thoughtfulness. Her eyes sparkled with suppressed excitement. When Hannah Gruen tried to learn the cause, she merely smiled.

"Tomorrow I expect to solve a great mystery," was all she would say.

Later, at the Woman's Club, Nancy's mood of dreamy anticipation persisted. It lent a warm glow to her skin. Helen Corning complimented her friend on her appearance.

"I've never seen you look prettier," she declared with sincerity. "The judges will be partial if they don't award you the grand prize tonight!"

"I feel as if I were walking in a dream," Nancy murmured. "Am I really taking part in this Fashion Show?"

"You certainly are!" Helen gave her friend a little shove toward the stage. "There is your cue now!"

Nancy glided gracefully down the carpeted stairway, treading as lightly as if upon air. Her blue eyes had a faraway look, her face an ethereal quality which caused many persons to whisper that she was beautiful.

Not a single misstep marred the girl's performance. She pivoted and turned, showing off the flowered Renaissance gown to the best advantage. The lovely, tiara-like headdress sparkled under the lights, adding the final touch to the exquisite costume. When at last Nancy returned to the wings, thunderous applause followed.

"You were superb, simply superb!" Helen exclaimed, giving her a hug.

Katherine praised Nancy, too, but she did not feel confident that the Renaissance gown would win the grand prize. Other costumes modeled in the show had received much attention. She was afraid that a white satin evening dress, created by a professional designer, Wilbur DeWolf, might be named by the judges.

Soon it was time for the all-important decisions to be announced. An expectant hush fell over the audience. Nancy joined the other models in crowding into the wings.

One of the judges made a little speech, praising all who had helped with the show. The audience stirred impatiently. Would the man never name the winners?

"And now, ladies and gentlemen," he rumbled in conclusion, "I take great pleasure in awarding the prizes. There are four; one for sport, one for daytime, and one for evening clothes, then the grand prize for the most artistic in the whole show."

Quickly he presented trophies for the sport and daytime dresses.

"And now, will Mr. Wilbur DeWolf please come forward. His design, modeled by——"

Nancy heard no more. Katherine had grabbed her hand, and a little sob had escaped from the foreign girl. She turned to start away, but was hemmed in by the crowd around her.

During the award the applause was tremendous. When it died down, the voice of the judge boomed out again.

"The grand prize—and may I say the vote of the committee was unanimous—goes to Miss

Katherine Kovna, designer of the Renaissance gown modeled by Miss Nancy Drew.''

He said more, but the words were drowned by hand clapping. Katherine, blinded by tears, hesitated. Quickly she dried her eyes and then appeared on the stage with Nancy. The foreign girl was so overcome with happiness that she could not speak other than to murmur, ''Thank you.''

Nancy, however, made a little speech for her, graciously acknowledging the honor paid them. Flash bulbs went off as photographers snapped pictures, and reporters pressed the girls for statements for the papers.

''I never was so happy in my life!'' Katherine declared, when at last the excitement was over. ''Now I sell many dresses and pay back all I owe Mr. Corning!''

''Don't worry about Dad,'' laughed Helen. ''You'll soon be making so much money at your frock shop that you'll wonder how you ever lacked customers.''

Nancy quickly changed into another dress, which could be worn on the straw ride.

''I hope Mr. Ellington meet us at the Inn,'' Katherine remarked wistfully. ''I do want him to know soon who won the big prize.''

The group of young people going to the supper and dance met at the ferry and crossed the river. A hayrack, pulled by two large, gray horses, awaited them on the opposite shore. Amid shouts of laughter they scrambled onto it.

Buck Rodman relieved the farmer of the

reins, and the horses started off at a fast clip. Bess began to sing a familiar song. The others joined in.

"Why so sober, Nancy?" Ned presently asked. He had noticed that she was not singing.

"Oh, just thinking," she replied. "Ned?"

"Yes."

"Will you do me a favor?"

"Just name it, and it's done."

"I have a very important task to be done. You're the person to help me."

"When do you want it done? Tonight?"

"No, tomorrow. I'll tell you all about it later on."

"O. K.," agreed Ned cheerfully. "We'll forget business now and feast our eyes on Old Man Moon."

An hour later Buck brought the hayrack safely into the parking lot of the Red Lion Inn. One by one the young people climbed out, brushing wisps of straw from their clothing.

"We're sights, but it's worth it!" George laughed, as she straightened her wind-blown hair. "And I'm as hungry as a bear!"

"Look who's here!" said Bess, giving Nancy a quick nudge.

Michael and another young man, whose face they could not see, crossed the parking lot. Nancy's heart began to beat excitedly.

"Where'd he come from?" George demanded in a whisper. "I hope he stays away from us. He's a pest!"

"We needn't pay any attention to him," Ned advised the others, as the two men entered the restaurant.

The young people trooped into the old Inn. It had been built in Revolutionary War days and was a long, brick building with a stone chimney at either end. The candle-lighted interior had been kept intact with all the furnishings of the Colonial period.

"What a delightful place for a party," exclaimed Katherine. "Now we find Mr. Ellington."

Ned inquired of the proprietor, and learned the artist had not arrived yet.

"That's odd," said Nancy. "We're late in arriving, too."

"Maybe he changed his plans at the last minute," Helen suggested, after they had waited for him nearly half an hour.

Katherine was very quiet, and the others realized that the sensitive girl was much embarrassed. She sat at the end of the long table, and twice Michael had come over to ask her to dance. She not only had refused, but changed seats to be near Nancy.

"I worry about Mr. Ellington," she said tensely.

"If I only knew his address, I could telephone," Nancy said thoughtfully.

Katherine volunteered the information that Mr. Ellington lived at an apartment house known as the Warrington Arms. She and Nancy left the room and sought a booth in the hall. A friend who lived with him answered the telephone.

"No, Mr. Ellington is not here," he assured Nancy. "When I last talked with him, he said he expected to go to the Red Lion Inn."

"How long ago was that?"

"About an hour ago. Mr. Ellington telephoned from Harbortown, saying he planned to go directly to the Inn."

Thanking the man for the information, Nancy hung up and turned to face her friend.

"He should have been here long ago," she said, growing more alarmed. "Harbortown is only a mile from here."

"What do you suppose happened to him?" cried Katherine, all the color fading from her cheeks.

"I can't imagine."

"Maybe his car run off the road—an accident!"

"I was thinking the same thing," Nancy replied quietly. "It seems to me that we should call the police without delay and find out."

CHAPTER XXI

NANCY IS WORRIED

NANCY returned to the telephone booth to call the police department. No accidents had been reported within the past hour, nor had anyone of Mr. Ellington's description figured in station reports.

"Guess I've worried unnecessarily," the girl thought in relief. "But it's strange that he should be delayed so long."

Opening the door of the glass-enclosed booth, Nancy was surprised to find Katherine had gone, but in a moment she knew why. She came face to face with Michael. She would have passed him with only a cold nod if he had not blocked her path.

"Miss Drew, may I say something to you?" he asked in a wheedling tone.

Nancy was surprised at the young man's change of attitude toward her. What did his sudden friendly overture mean? Many ideas of what she ought to do came into her mind, but she decided to listen to him first.

"I want to apologize for the way I've acted," he went on. "I said some things I didn't mean."

"I'll accept your apology," Nancy replied noncommittally.

"We ought to be good friends. Grandmother wants it that way."

"Yes, I guess she does," Nancy agreed. After a pause she added, "Suppose I come to the house tomorrow to tea. Will you be there?"

"Tomorrow? Uh—no—yes," he stammered. "I—I had some business to attend to, but I'll put it off."

Nancy felt sure the man had some ulterior motive for being so polite and friendly.

"Grandmother thinks I'm the tops now," Michael resumed. "She'll keep on thinking that, if Anna will just mind her own business."

"What has Anna to do with it?"

"Oh, that old busybody keeps telling Grandmother not to give me money. I have to baby Anna along all the time to keep her in good humor. Why don't you put in a good word for me?"

Nancy smiled, realizing now why the man had adopted such a cordial attitude. He had been building up to this request.

"So you think I have influence with Anna?" she inquired.

"Sure, whatever you say goes with her. How about it?"

"We'll see," Nancy replied vaguely. "Be sure to be at home tomorrow afternoon."

Before Michael could continue the conversation, she moved past him and rejoined her

friends. Katherine Kovna and everyone else
was relieved to hear that Mr. Ellington had not
figured in an accident, but the young dress designer's evening was spoiled. The others were
very kind to her, and the boys saw to it that
she danced a great deal. While Nancy and
Ned were waltzing together, he asked his partner what her idea was about Mr. Ellington not
making an appearance.

"I'm really worried that something has happened to him," she replied. "He's too much
of a gentleman not to have sent word."

"Well, if he wasn't in an accident, what
could have happened to him?" Ned persisted.

"Lots of things. Thieves could have waylaid
him, knocked him out, and stolen his car."

"Gee, you're cheerful. What else?"

"Maybe he didn't use a car. He might have
been walking along the river road and fallen."

"Then let's get out of here and go look for
him," Ned suggested.

He had no idea they would find the missing
artist, but he was glad of an excuse to walk in
the moonlight with Nancy. As they followed
the road that wound in and out along the river,
the youth felt only the romance of the evening.
But Nancy's thoughts, already full of mystery,
turned to the eeriness of the night scene. A
cool breeze blew from the water, moving the
low-hanging tree branches. Now and then the
moon would bury itself in a cloud, causing gro-
tesque shadows to flicker across their path.

"Ned, what was that?"

Nancy stopped short, gripping his arm.

"Where?" he demanded, puzzled. "I didn't see or hear anything."

"I saw a figure hiding behind that giant pine tree," she whispered. "We're being followed."

"Why should anyone follow us? Come on," he urged, not wishing to return yet. "You want to find Ellington, don't you?"

Somewhat dubiously, Nancy allowed herself to be led on down the road. Ned did not know she had been threatened, and that she had promised her father she would be careful.

She kept her gaze fastened on the line of trees. Suddenly another moving shadow appeared, and this time Nancy was certain it had been made by a human form.

"Ned," she whispered, "I'm sure we're being spied upon!"

"I'll soon find out!"

The youth started toward the trees, but Nancy pulled him back.

"Don't be rash," she cautioned. "We're in a lonely locality, far from any help. We're in danger. I can't explain more now, but we must go right back."

Quickly she turned and began to run, Ned at her heels. Not until she was within the rays of light from the Inn did she slow down to a walk.

"Now tell me what the rush was for," panted Ned.

"Something of tremendous importance is at stake. I don't trust Michael, and I feel his be-

ing here tonight is to establish an alibi. I believe I ought to carry out a plan right away
that I was going to do tomorrow."

"The one you wanted me to help you with?"

"Yes. You go get Buck and wait here for
me. I'll locate our victim!" she replied tensely.

Scarcely had Ned vanished into the Inn than
Nancy saw a lone man coming hurriedly along
the river road. For an instant she wondered
if he were Mr. Ellington. But as he drew
closer, she recognized Michael's companion.
Not wishing him to see her, she ducked behind
a lilac bush.

"He must be the one who followed Ned and
me!" she decided.

The man passed close to where the girl
crouched. Without seeing her, he entered the
Inn by a side door.

"I'll follow and find out what he tells
Michael!" Nancy determined.

Entering the hallway of the Inn, she saw him
go into the dining room. She was about to follow when from a half-closed telephone booth
she heard a familiar voice.

"Everything's going as we planned," she
distinguished the words, spoken in a mocking
tone. "Yes, I'm with your friend Nancy Drew
now. Sure, I'm watching things. How's my
dear grandma, ha, ha?"

Nancy moved closer, but she heard no more.
Michael lowered his voice, and a moment later
came from the telephone booth.

"Now what was the significance of that

conversation?" the bewildered girl thought. "Surely Michael couldn't have been talking to Anna."

"He's up to something!" she thought with growing excitement. "The sooner I carry out my plan the better."

With no suspicion that he was being observed, Michael started to return to the dining room. Quickly Nancy walked up to him.

"Wouldn't you like to join some of us in the garden?" she asked sweetly.

The young man looked surprised but accepted the invitation. Nancy suggested he wait for her by a little pool. He went outside just as Ned returned with Helen and Buck.

"How would you like to expose an impostor?" Nancy whispered.

"What!" said the three in unison.

"Anything you say," Buck agreed with a grin.

"I believe the man known as Michael Alexandra is not a prince," whispered Nancy tensely. "But we'll know in a minute."

"What do you want us to do?" asked Buck.

"How are you at kidnaping?"

"Expert," grinned Ned. "When do we nab him? Now?"

"Yes, but it must be a neat, noiseless job. We'll all walk down to the pool where Michael is waiting. Then when I give the signal, overpower him and I'll tell you what to do."

"The job suits me to a 'T,'" Buck declared grimly. "Come on, let's go!"

"Remember, it must be a quiet job," Nancy warned. "If he lets out a yell, everything will be spoiled."

"Leave it to us!" Ned replied. "I've been wanting to do something to that fellow ever since the boat ride."

The young people wandered out into the garden. They paused at the pool, forming a circle about the unsuspecting Michael. Then at a signal from Nancy, Buck and Ned closed in from the rear.

Before the captive could make a sound, they had covered his mouth. Lifting him bodily, they dragged him behind some bushes. No one would be apt to notice them in that spot, but there was enough light from a near-by lamp for them to see. Nancy spoke up quickly.

"If you will act like a gentleman and not yell for help, we'll allow you to talk," she told him.

"One yip out of you, and you'll get rough treatment!" Ned warned the man, removing his hand from the young man's mouth.

"What's the idea?" Michael demanded furiously. "I'll have you know you can't treat me like this! Why, I'm a prince——"

"How can you prove it?" Nancy demanded.

"With papers. You took them to Grandmother yourself!"

"I gave her certain proofs—yes. But how do I know where you obtained them? They may have belonged to another person."

"That's a lie," Michael mumbled, struggling

hard to break away from Ned and Buck.

"I have good reason to believe that you are an impostor," Nancy resumed coolly. "I know that you have been robbing your grandmother."

"You can't prove a thing! You're only bluffing!"

"Am I?"

"Grandmother is satisfied that I am the lost prince."

"If you're the missing Michael, you can prove your identity right now," Nancy retorted.

"I don't know what you're talking about," he protested savagely.

"You will in a moment," Nancy smiled as she turned to Ned and Buck. "Boys," she requested, enjoying the situation to the full, "will you please remove this man's shoes and socks at once?"

CHAPTER XXII

A PRINCE

"SAY, what's the big idea?" Michael protested furiously. "You can't take off my shoes!"

"Oh, can't we?" mocked Buck Rodman. "Well, just watch!"

While their captive struggled and fought, he and Ned stripped off the shoes and socks.

"I wish I had a flashlight," Nancy sighed.

"Here's one in the prince's pocket," Ned said sarcastically, offering it to her.

To the surprise of the young people Nancy flashed the light directly on the soles of Michael's bare feet.

"Just as I thought!" she exclaimed, and added, "You are not Mrs. Alexandra's long-lost grandson! You are an impostor!"

"That's not true," the young man whined. "Why are you looking at my feet?"

"If you actually were Michael Alexandra, you would know the answer without asking!"

"You're just trying to cheat me out of my inheritance."

Nancy was stern as she faced the captive. "You'll never obtain another penny from Mrs. Alexandra! Your little game has ended."

"Why do you say I am not the prince?"

"I shan't tell you that, but I have absolute proof. You may as well confess."

Michael stared sullenly at the little group. Nancy was convinced he never would talk. Therefore, it came as a surprise when he muttered:

"O. K., I'll admit I'm not Michael Alexandra."

"Where did you obtain your so-called credentials?" Nancy asked sternly. "I mean the letter and picture and toy?"

"Found 'em on a train seat, coming into River Heights."

"Then the real Prince Michael may be somewhere near here!" Nancy exclaimed, thinking aloud. She turned to the prisoner. "Where is he?"

"I don't know who the guy is, or where he went," the man insisted sullenly.

"What's your real name?" the girl asked.

Michael would not reply. Not suspecting that the police were to be summoned, he sat down on the ground, waiting for a chance to escape from the boys.

Nancy went into the Inn and telephoned headquarters. Then she spoke to the others at the table, asking two of the young men to locate Michael's companion. He could not be found anywhere, and Nancy assumed he had got wind of what was going on and left. A police cruiser soon arrived at the grounds and took away the prisoner.

"Let's go inside," Helen proposed after the vehicle had disappeared down the road. "Then suppose you tell us, Nancy, just how you knew about the identification of the lost prince."

"It was the Clue in the Jewel Box," her chum replied. "Later I'll tell you just what it is, but in this public place I'm afraid someone else like Michael might hear me."

Nancy followed the others toward the Inn. She had gone only a short distance before she paused, obviously disturbed.

"Something else wrong?" Ned inquired.

"I can't help feeling worried about Mrs. Alexandra and Anna," she confessed, frowning.

"With the impostor in the hands of the police, they should be safer than before."

"That's just the point, Ned. That man is a clever thief, and he may have accomplices."

"Even so, his pals wouldn't have been likely to make trouble for Mrs. Alexandra with him out here, would they?"

"I'm not so sure of that. He is the one known to us, so he would have to establish an alibi. Ned, I heard him talking over the telephone a little while ago. I thought at first it might have been to Anna, but some of his remarks didn't sound right."

"What did he say?" the youth asked.

" 'Everything's fine. I'm with your friend Nancy Drew. Sure, I'm watching things. And how's my dear grandma?' "

"That does sound sort of odd."

"He asked, 'How's my dear grandma?' rather mockingly," Nancy went on. "Almost as if he knew she might be in trouble."

"You don't think any of the fellow's pals are at the Alexandra house tonight?"

"That's just what I'm afraid of, Ned. When I learned what the Clue in the Jewel Box was, I advised Mrs. Alexandra not to give her grandson any more jewels or art objects to sell. If she acted on my suggestion, then he probably realized his little game was nearing an end."

"And figured he had to clean up fast?"

"That's the way I look at it, Ned. He may have arranged for his pals to rob the house this very night. I overheard Michael tell Anna he probably wouldn't be home, and when I asked him if he'd be there tomorrow, he stammered and seemed uncertain at first."

"If he were seen here, then he couldn't possibly be blamed," added Ned. "Say, his pals may be robbing Mrs. Alexandra at this very minute!"

"Let's see what we can find out on the telephone!"

The two young people hurried to a booth. Many times they called the former queen's residence, but there was no answer.

"Something must be wrong!" Nancy declared, firmly convinced. "Mrs. Alexandra and Anna almost never leave the house at night."

"Shall we tell the police to go there?"

"I'd rather go myself," the girl replied.

"We can take a taxi. If everything is all right, I'd be very embarrassed sending the police for nothing."

"I'll ask Buck to come along with us," Ned said, hanging up the telephone receiver. "If there's any trouble, we could use a little of his muscle."

Buck was more than willing to accompany the couple, and Katherine insisted upon going along. They found an empty cab parked near the door of the Inn.

"Make all speed to the ferry!" Ned urged him.

"If we miss the boat, there won't be another along for half an hour," Buck added, glancing at his wrist watch. "We have just ten minutes to make it."

"I'll get you there," the man assured them.

Exactly ten minutes later the taxi arrived at the dock. An instant before the gates were lowered, the cab drove aboard. The ride across the river consumed its usual time, but to Nancy it seemed hours before the boat touched the opposite shore.

"Now to 47 Downing Street!" she urged the driver, as the cab rolled off the runway.

Through the streets the car sped, drawing up at last before the house. Not a light shone in any of the windows.

"Everything looks all right," said Katherine.

"I'll feel much better when I'm sure nothing has happened," replied Nancy, alighting.

Buck paid the cab driver, and the young people went up the walk. Ned rang the doorbell.

"Try again," Katherine urged, when there was no response from within the house.

Again Ned pressed the button, holding his finger on it for a long while.

"That's enough to wake anybody," he declared.

"I'm going inside," said Nancy. "I wonder if all the doors are locked."

"This one is," Buck reported, testing the knob.

Circling the house, the young people tried the rear door. It too was locked, but Ned scrambled up a trellis to a high pantry window. The sash raised without difficulty. Crawling through, he found the back door and unlocked it.

"The house is certainly quiet," he reported in a whisper. "If the neighbors see us, they may report us as burglars."

"We can explain why we are here," Nancy replied, boldly switching on lights as she walked through to the living room.

When this place became illuminated, the young people were appalled by the sight which met their gaze. Expensive hangings had been stripped from the walls. Tapestry coverings were gone from the chairs. All the art objects were missing.

"The house has been ransacked!" Nancy exclaimed. "I was afraid of that!"

"What has become of Mrs. Alexandra and

Anna?" Katherine cried, picking up a torn white apron from the floor.

"I'll look upstairs," said Nancy.

She started up the dark stairway, calling the names of the women. There was no answer.

Buck and Ned followed close behind her, groping for an electric switch. From the floor above they thought they heard a low moaning sound.

"There must be a light here somewhere," Nancy murmured, inching her way along the upper hall.

The next instant she stumbled over a body lying on the carpet.

"Ned! Buck!" she called, as she bent over the inert form.

CHAPTER XXIII

A ROBBERY

JUST as Nancy shouted that she had found someone lying on the floor, Ned's groping fingers located the electric light switch at the top of the stairs. He pressed the button.

"It's Anna!" Nancy gasped, recognizing the motionless figure. "Bound and gagged!"

Katherine raced up the stairs. With a penknife Ned severed the cords and removed the handkerchief from the servant's mouth. Even then she showed no sign of regaining consciousness.

"She's in a faint," Nancy said anxiously. "Get some water from the bathroom, Katherine."

Leaving the others to look after Anna, she hurried into Mrs. Alexandra's bedroom. Her worst fears were confirmed. The old lady lay face downward upon the bed. Her hands and feet were tightly bound with clothesline, and a cloth had been stuffed into her mouth. Nancy jerked off the gag.

"Mrs. Alexandra, speak to me!" she pleaded. "It's Nancy!"

The old lady's eyelids fluttered open and

then closed again. She lapsed into unconsciousness.

"Mrs. Alexandra is in a serious condition," Nancy said, as Ned quickly cut the leg and arm cords. "She may have had another heart attack. We'd better call a doctor."

Buck appeared in the doorway, carrying Anna. Carefully he laid her on the bed beside her mistress.

Nancy ran downstairs. Fortunately, the telephone wire had not been cut, and she was able to summon a doctor. He arrived ten minutes later. The physician examined Anna briefly but spent a much longer time with Mrs. Alexandra.

"These women both require expert nursing care," he said soberly after giving them mild heart stimulants. "Mrs. Alexandra is in a serious condition."

"She'll not die?" Nancy gasped, thoroughly alarmed.

"That I cannot say," the doctor replied. "Her heart is very weak."

"In that case, I wonder if it might not be best to take both women to the hospital?" Nancy asked after a moment of thought. "There is no one here to take care of them. Besides, Mrs. Alexandra will be dreadfully upset when she learns that her home has been robbed."

"Then you think she is unaware of what happened?" the doctor questioned in surprise.

"She may not have seen her attacker, or

suspected why he came here. Also, if she remains, she will ask to see Michael.''

''Who is he?''

''A man who posed as her grandson. He was arrested tonight. So far she knows nothing of it.''

''Then by all means I advise hospital care,'' the doctor said quickly. ''I will make the necessary arrangements now.''

While the physician occupied himself at the telephone, Nancy sent Buck to summon the police. She and Katherine remained with Mrs. Alexandra and Anna, while Ned explored the house. Presently the doctor came back upstairs.

''The ambulance will be here soon,'' he reported, pulling a chair to the bedside. ''I will stay until it arrives.''

Relieved of responsibility, Nancy took time to inspect the house. As she had feared, almost everything of value except heavy pieces of furniture had been stolen. The Footman jewel case was gone, the Easter egg, a pair of gold candlesticks, the silverware—everything that Mrs. Alexandra treasured.

''The poor woman never will survive this blow,'' Nancy said sadly to Ned. ''How can we ever tell her the truth?''

''Maybe the police can get some of the things back,'' he returned hopefully.

Within a few minutes a car arrived from headquarters. Nancy was able to give the officers a detailed description of nearly every object which had been stolen from the house.

"Any idea who committed the crime?" the policeman asked her.

"Indeed I have!" she responded. "The theft probably was engineered by the same man whom I had arrested tonight on the other side of the river. I don't know his real name—he wouldn't tell me. He has been living here, posing as a relative, and robbing Mrs. Alexandra."

"Then the actual robbery must have been done by one or more of his pals," the officer added. "Mrs. Alexandra hasn't talked?"

"No, neither she nor her servant has been able to say a word."

"We may get something out of them after they recover from shock," the policeman declared. "In the meantime, we'll work on the prisoner and try to make him identify his friends."

Soon after the men had completed their inspection of the house, the hospital ambulance arrived. Nancy rode to the institution, remaining at Mrs. Alexandra's bedside even after a nurse had been assigned to take care of her.

"I want to be here in case she should recover consciousness," Nancy explained. "She may say something that will help to make an arrest."

The girl was allowed to remain. Katherine took up her post in another room beside Anna's bed. Now and then she and Nancy would meet in the hall to hold whispered consultations.

"Anna—she spoke a little while ago," Katherine reported at one of the sessions. "She's causing the nurse much worry."

"What does she say?" Nancy asked eagerly.

"She keep mumbling about a jewel box being stolen."

"Then she must know what happened. Katherine, at the next opportunity try to get her to describe the man who bound her."

"I learn what I can," the girl promised soberly.

Nancy returned to Mrs. Alexandra's bedside. A moment later the nurse excused herself to attend to an errand in another part of the hospital. The sound of the closing door seemed to arouse the patient from her long stupor. She opened her eyes, staring at Nancy without recognition.

"No! No!" she whispered, clutching the bed clothes. "Do not strike me! I will tell you where my money is hidden!"

"Mrs. Alexandra, you are all right now," Nancy quieted her. "Don't you know me? I am Nancy Drew."

Mrs. Alexandra relaxed slightly. She reached for the girl's hand, clinging tightly to it.

"My jewels—" she whispered.

"Now don't worry about anything," Nancy comforted the woman. "The police will get your money back for you."

"Then that was all they took—the money from my purse?"

Nancy did not answer the question, and the patient seemed to forget that she had asked it.

With a deep sigh, she closed her eyes again.

"Mrs. Alexandra," Nancy said, fearing that the woman would lapse into a stupor once more, "did you see the man who tied you up?"

"I was upstairs alone when he came into the room," Mrs. Alexandra replied, speaking with great difficulty. "The man wore a black mask."

"Was he tall or short?"

"Short. He wore a brown suit. That's all I remember."

Before Nancy could ask another question, Katherine appeared in the doorway. She motioned for the girl to come out into the hall.

"Anna has talked to me!" she said as Nancy joined her. "She tell me that she was in the library when she hear a noise. As she step into the living room to investigate, a masked man leap at her. They struggle, she break away and run upstairs toward Mrs. Alexandra's room. Just then another man step out and grab her. That is all she can remember."

"Then there must have been at least two men in the house," Nancy responded gravely. "Was Anna able to describe either of them?"

"She say one upstairs have coal black eyes and wear a dark suit. Oh, yes, she call him a very short, stubby man."

"That tallies with Mrs. Alexandra's description," Nancy said thoughtfully. "I wonder if by any chance he may be a certain pickpocket the police are looking for? He may be part of a big thieving ring, as well as a specialist in picking pockets."

Convinced that the clue was a vital one, she waited until the nurse returned to take charge, then she sought a public telephone. Calling police headquarters, she repeated the information received from the two patients. To her satisfaction, the desk sergeant promised that a special effort would be made to round up the long-sought pickpocket at once.

The hour was late, and Nancy knew that Hannah Gruen and Carson Drew would be worried. She decided to telephone to them, and was just about to call when Ned thrust his head into the booth.

"Spare your nickel if you're calling home," he advised cheerfully. "I talked to your father about ten minutes ago. He says for you to stay here as long as you are needed."

"That's fine," Nancy declared in relief. "I may as well go home, though. There's nothing more I can do here."

"Let's get Katherine and Buck, and go somewhere to eat," Ned proposed quickly.

"I am half starved," Nancy admitted. "We cheated ourselves out of most of the supper at the Inn. But what about the party there? Shouldn't Buck go back and get Helen?"

"He phoned when we first got here, and the party was breaking up then. Hal and Midge were going to take Helen home."

When Katherine heard this, she consented to go with the others, and the four young people left the hospital.

"Where to?" Ned asked.

"Not many places open at this time of night," Buck responded, glancing up and down the deserted street. "I know a diner that has good food, but it's not much for style."

"Lead on," encouraged Ned. "All we ask is food, and plenty of it!"

Buck escorted the party to a place that was open all night. It had no customers save a truck driver, who sat at the counter drinking a cup of coffee.

"I believe I may as well order breakfast," Nancy declared, scanning the menu. "Orange juice, waffles——"

She broke off, for the door had opened. Into the diner had come a short man who breathed hard from hurrying. Almost at his heels trailed a policeman.

"Hold on there!" the officer exclaimed, catching the fellow by an arm. "I've got you this time!"

"You've made a stupid mistake," the accused one replied in a haughty voice. "Frequently I am taken for a pickpocket who closely resembles me."

"Well, we're looking for him, too."

"But my name is Dorrance."

"Doesn't mean a thing to me."

Dorrance's gaze roved about the diner and came to rest upon Nancy. His eyes brightened.

"Here's a young lady who knows me well, and knows I'm honest," he told the officer.

Smiling at the girl, he took a handkerchief from his vest pocket and waved it.

"Can you identify this man?" the policeman asked the girl.

"Indeed, I can."

Nancy arose and faced David Dorrance.

"Just tell him who I am," the young man requested gleefully.

Nancy turned to the officer. "Arrest this man!" she said, her words dropping like chips of steel. "He is one of the two pickpockets the police are looking for!"

CHAPTER XXIV

NANCY'S ACCUSATION

DAVID DORRANCE stared at Nancy as if unable to believe his ears. He had felt certain that she would exonerate him, and instead she had accused him of being wanted by the police.

"Just because I look like another man is no reason for arresting me as a thief," he protested vigorously.

"I suggested to the police some time ago that you be picked up for questioning," she told him. "If you are innocent, you won't mind submitting to a search."

At this remark the color drained from the man's face. The officer examined his pockets, which held a large sum of money. One of the greenbacks was a marked bill the police department had used as bait.

"Guess you're one of the fellows we're looking for, all right," the officer remarked. "Come along."

"All right, you win," said Dorrance, glancing angrily at Nancy. "Tell me, Miss Drew, just how you figured this all out."

"Some time ago I decided that you and your double work together. One of you picks the

193

pocket of a victim, and either makes a quick
getaway, or passes the loot to your friend
through a window or a door. Then the other
plays innocent, and of course the pocketbook is
never found on him.''

''Quite a theory!'' Mr. Dorrance sneered.

''It took me a little while to figure it out,''
Nancy resumed, unruffled. ''That clever handkerchief scheme proved your undoing. For a
long time it fooled me—then one day you gave
yourself away.''

''How was that?'' Dorrance demanded.

''By waving it once too often. You and your
pal robbed Mr. Faber. In escaping, your
friend nearly forgot to wave his handkerchief
at me. Then a moment later you tried the same
stunt. It didn't take any great power of deduc-
tion to figure that you couldn't have moved
from the office building to the store in such a
short time!''

''I didn't think you'd be clever enough to
figure it out!'' said the thief, and was led away.

Forgetting how hungry they were, the young
people decided to follow the prisoner to the
police station. Nancy wished to hear what else
Dorrance might confess, and learn what she
could about the prisoner who had posed as Mrs.
Alexandra's grandson.

At the station, Nancy repeated everything
she knew about the two crooks. Under questioning, Dorrance admitted his part of the
thievery, acknowledging that he had stolen
Carson Drew's wallet and had fleeced many

other persons. His double, he said, was a professional pickpocket. They had met accidentally, and thought out the little scheme they had been working. When he would not tell the fellow's name, Nancy spoke up.

"Isn't it Jim Cordova?"

The prisoner's look of surprise was enough of a confession. "I suppose that woman in the apartment house on Water Street talked too much," he said. "Jim's related to her husband."

"One day you locked me in the phone booth there, and he jumped out the window, didn't he?"

"You're too smart," said Dorrance.

"Where is your double now?" he was questioned.

"That's for you to find out!" Dorrance retorted sullenly.

"Don't worry, we'll round him up," the police lieutenant assured him.

In addition to the money in Dorrance's pockets, a little notebook was found. It contained two addresses; that of a house on Clayton Avenue, and the Alexandra residence.

"The Clayton Avenue place may be Cordova's hide-out," declared the officer. "We'll search there at once. Now I wonder about this Alexandra address."

"The man arrested at the Red Lion Inn tonight lived there," Nancy explained eagerly. "It's my theory that he was associated with Dorrance and Cordova. I believe that the

three of them planned the robbery at Mrs.
Alexandra's.''

"We'll soon know," replied the lieutenant.
"It shouldn't take us long to round up Cordova."

It was so late that Nancy and her friends did
not remain longer at the police station. However, the next morning they learned by telephone that a successful raid had been staged at
the Clayton Avenue house. Although Cordova
had not been captured, nearly all of Mrs. Alexandra's jewels and antiques were recovered, as
well as valuable papers belonging to Carson
Drew.

"This is wonderful, Dad!" Nancy cried, as
she sat down to breakfast with her father and
repeated the information to him. "You'll get
back all the money that was stolen from you,
perhaps."

"That'll be a load off my mind," Mr. Drew
sighed. "Nancy, I'm proud of the way you
handled this mystery. You did it without danger to yourself, as you promised me you
would."

"But as to the Clue in the Jewel Box—well,
I'm right back where I started from. Prince
Michael still has not been found."

Mr. Drew smiled. "You're always a little
uneasy after you solve a mystery, until you find
another one. So this time one overlaps the
other."

"I have a good clue to work on in hunting
for Mrs. Alexandra's grandson," said his

daughter. "If he is alive, then it ought to be easy to——"

Suddenly a voice boomed through the front screen door, calling "Carson, where are you?"

The lawyer glanced at his watch. "My goodness, Nancy, it's after nine o'clock. That's Mr. Field out there. Promised to meet him twenty minutes ago. I must be off. Good-by, dear. Take it easy today."

He kissed her affectionately and left the house. Nancy immediately telephoned the hospital and learned that Mrs. Alexandra and Anna were somewhat improved. The latter, at least, would be able to return home the following day.

"Now I believe I'll find out if Katherine has heard from Mr. Ellington," Nancy decided.

She called the young designer at her shop, and learned that the artist had not communicated with the girl.

"Oh, Nancy, I worry," the young woman said. "He is so kind, such a gentleman, I do not see how he could—what you say, break a date with me. But I cannot find out myself, for perhaps he changed his mind."

"I'll call his apartment," offered Nancy.

The same man who had answered the evening before told her Ellington had not come home, nor had he sent any word.

"He has an appointment at nine this morning, but he is not here for it," his friend added.

Lost in thought, Nancy put down the telephone. What could have become of the artist?

"He may come any minute, so I shan't worry too much yet," she decided.

She walked over to the police station to gather more information about the two prisoners in whom she was interested. She learned that during the night the impostor prince, whose real name was Brandette, had signed a confession.

It definitely implicated him in the robbery at the Alexandra home. According to his own story, he had met the two pickpockets, Dorrance and Cordova, quite by accident when they had stolen his wallet.

"Brandette was a small-time thief himself. He caught on at once to the way the pickpockets' scheme worked, and told Dorrance so," explained the lieutenant. "Dorrance immediately whistled in a certain way, so his pal would drop the stolen wallet."

"That was the first time I saw the three of them," said Nancy.

"Brandette professed admiration for the pickpockets' work, with the result that the three men became pals, and planned how to rob Mrs. Alexandra after one of them had gone there to live."

"So the impostor wasn't keeping all the money that came from the sale of the jewels," said Nancy.

"No, the pickpockets were helping him dispose of the articles as fast as seemed safe, and taking most of the money received for them. Then you came along and spoiled their scheme!"

The officer gave Nancy a warm smile, and she blushed at his praise.

"Brandette and Dorrance threatened you outside your home one night," he explained, "but didn't stop your work. So they decided to loot the Alexandra home last night," he concluded.

"They nearly succeeded, too," Nancy commented. "When I think what might have happened to Mrs. Alexandra and Anna, the shivers run down my spine."

"Your timely arrival at the house last night undoubtedly saved their lives," praised the lieutenant. "Not to mention the property."

"Has everything been recovered?" the girl inquired.

"Very nearly," replied the officer, consulting a memorandum. "Most of the jewels were brought in last night. My men will haul away the remaining pieces this morning."

"What will be done with the things?" Nancy asked thoughtfully.

"We'll have to hold 'em here until Mrs. Alexandra can identify them."

"She may be in the hospital for several days. I was wondering—couldn't I do it for Mrs. Alexandra? Then the things could be taken to her home, and everything fixed up again."

"I think it can be arranged," nodded the lieutenant. "Can you identify the pieces?"

"A good many of them."

"Then I'll have you go over the things."

As Nancy went to inspect the loot, which had been brought into the station, she asked the officer if Brandette had volunteered any information about the real Prince Michael.

"I don't think he knows anything," the lieutenant replied. "According to his confession, he found an art portfolio left by a man sitting in front of him on a train."

"An art portfolio?" Nancy repeated meditatively.

"Yes, Brandette inspected its contents. Discovering that the photograph and letter which it contained might lead to a fortune, he decided to keep the property. His first act was to take the name of Francis Baum. From letters in the portfolio he knew this was the one given the prince by his nurse. Evidently the woman was afraid that if Michael should use his real name, enemies might harm him."

"Did Brandette describe the man who sat in front of him?" Nancy asked after a moment.

"No, he refuses to give any information on that point."

"Yet he must remember the person," Nancy said musingly. "I suppose he resents the fact that another man is entitled to fill his shoes as the true prince. By the way, did he mention a Mr. Ellington?"

"Ellington? No, I am quite sure he did not."

Nancy's mind was racing. Could it be possible that it was Ellington's portfolio Brandette had picked up? The artist might be the lost prince! And if not, he probably knew who that person was!

"The impostor certainly acted as if he didn't want Mr. Ellington to see him that day out on the river," the girl thought. "Oh, I must get in touch with the artist right away!"

Nancy was brought out of her reverie by a surprising remark from the police officer.

"Brandette made an admission in regard to you. He said that he overheard you at the telephone making plans for a party at the Red Lion Inn. That was why he went there, to his sorrow."

"I believe he had a double reason for appearing at the Inn," Nancy returned slowly. "Obviously he wanted me to see him in order to establish an alibi for the Alexandra robbery. But that doesn't explain why his companion trailed a friend of mine and me along the river road."

"We'll keep working on him," the officer promised. "He may do some more talking."

As soon as Nancy left the police station, she telephoned to Ellington's apartment only to learn that no word had come from the man. Absently she helped her chums put the Alexandra home in order. As the others worked, they discussed ways and means of locating the real Prince Michael, but Nancy said little.

"He must be somewhere in River Heights," Bess declared, holding a tapestry for George to tack into place. "If only I knew what he looks like!"

"We might try communicating with various hospitals and schools," suggested Helen Corning. She was carefully replacing bric-a-brac in a cupboard. "Nancy, why are you so quiet?"

"I'm worried about Mr. Ellington," the girl replied.

"That's right!" exclaimed Bess. "No one has heard a word from him since he agreed to meet us at the Inn."

"Just as soon as we finish putting this house in order," said Nancy, "I propose that, if he hasn't returned, we get Ned and some of the other boys, and start a search for him."

"Good idea," agreed Bess.

"Are the police going to bring everything back here?" asked George. "If so, there ought to be someone on guard when we leave," she added practically.

"You're right," said Nancy.

She called the station house and found that they could not send a man until five o'clock, but he would stay overnight.

"I guess it will take us until five to fix up this place," said Helen.

About half past four Katherine Kovna came to the Alexandra residence, and praised the girls' work. Rather diffidently she asked Nancy if Mr. Ellington had returned. Upon learning that the girl had just made another fruitless telephone call to the artist's apartment, she became quite excited.

"Oh, he must be in trouble!" she cried.
"We must do something!"

"A search is to be started in half an hour,"
said Nancy. "Of course you'll join us."

"Yes, yes. Where do we go?"

"To the Red Lion Inn."

"You think we may find a what-you-call
'clue' there?" Katherine asked, her face
brightening.

"That's my hope. Mr. Ellington disappeared
somewhere between Harbortown and that restaurant."

By the time the policeman arrived, the girls
had the entire residence in order once more.
Mrs. Alexandra's precious stones had been returned to the Footman jewel box, and every
art object was in its former place.

"If only we could find the true Prince Michael, the lovely queen mother's homecoming
would be a happy one," Katherine sighed, as
the four friends left the house.

Immediately after a hasty dinner at the Inn,
the group of girls, with Ned, Buck, and three
other boys, started out to hunt for Mr. Ellington. Learning that there were two roads between Harbortown and the Red Lion Inn, they
decided to form two searching parties. Nancy,
Ned, Katherine, and a Tom White decided to
follow the river route, while the others would
try the higher road.

"It's getting dark," Ned remarked before
they had gone far. "Too bad we didn't start
earlier."

Nancy nodded as she tested the beam of a flashlight. The moon would not rise for many hours. She had not realized that it would grow dark so soon.

"Say, what's that over in those bushes?" Ned suddenly demanded about fifteen minutes later. "Looks like a parked car!"

Scrambling through the underbrush, the young people reached the automobile. It was a gray coupé of a late model.

"Oh, this is Mr. Ellington's car!" Katherine cried, fairly beside herself with nervousness. "What has happened? Maybe he jump in the river!"

"Ellington's been waylaid—that's what happened!" Ned exclaimed, jerking open the car door. "Here's his hat lying on the seat."

"There's been a struggle!" Nancy added, flashing her light over the ground. "See! The grass has been trampled. And a body has been dragged over the ground!"

"Which way does the trail lead?" Ned demanded, losing interest in the car.

"This way—toward the river."

"Oh! Oh! Maybe he was thrown in the water!" Katherine shuddered, clutching Nancy's hand.

The trail of footsteps and trampled grass led down a steep slope to the very bank of the river. A little distance away stood an abandoned boathouse whose weakened posts threatened to give way beneath it. As Nancy flashed her

light over the building, she thought she heard
a faint cry.

"Listen!" she whispered tensely.

"Help! Help!" came a weak, pathetic call.

It was hard to tell whether the sound had
come from inside or outside the boathouse.

"Let's go!" Ned cried, starting forward.
"Ellington may be locked up in there!"

He and the girls headed for a door to the
building, but Tom took a path which led around
the far side of the structure. Before the three
who were together reached the water's edge,
a strange voice boomed at them from the darkness.

"Come no nearer or take the consequence!"

As the trio halted, they again heard the feeble call for help.

"What shall we do?" Katherine whispered
nervously. "If we go on, maybe we be shot!"

CHAPTER XXV

Two Mysteries Solved

As the weak cry for help was repeated, Ned switched on his flashlight, pointing its bright beam at the old boathouse. A man was standing on a narrow platform facing them.

"Ned! That fellow is the pickpocket wanted by the police!" Nancy whispered tensely. "Dorrance's double!"

"Has he a gun?"

"I can't see one."

"Then I'm going to try to nab him," muttered Ned, putting out his flashlight and handing it to Nancy. "When I shout, train this right in his eyes!"

"Be careful," Katherine warned anxiously.

Crouching low behind some bushes, Ned moved a little distance down the shore. In the darkness the man on the boathouse platform could see only Nancy's light, which she was playing over the trees.

Suddenly a board creaked, there was a shout, and a flashlight was turned full on his face. The pickpocket whirled around, but Ned leaped on him, and the two went down together.

Nancy and Katherine ran to assist. The pickpocket did not give up without a violent struggle, but the young people quickly subdued him.

"You hold him while I look inside the boathouse," Nancy urged Ned.

Followed by Katherine, she opened the creaking door to the old building.

"Mr. Ellington!" she called softly. "Are you here?"

From deep within the building came a low moan. But before the girls could investigate they heard a wild yell from Ned. The sound of scuffling feet told them that the prisoner was trying to escape.

Darting back to the platform, Nancy and Katherine were dismayed to see the man streaking down the beach. Ned pursued him, but it was unlikely he could overtake the thief.

"Oh, if that isn't the worst break!" Nancy exclaimed, and then ended with a shriek of joy.

Tom White had grabbed the fellow suddenly. In a moment Ned arrived to help subdue their captive. Nancy and Katherine, their minds relieved, resumed their search in the boathouse.

"Help! Help!" the feeble cry was repeated.

"It may be a trap to get us in here, but I don't think so," Nancy whispered in warning to her companion.

Cautiously the girls moved forward, flashing their two lights over the half-rotted flooring. Katherine squealed as her hand brushed against a thick cobweb. Both she and Nancy jumped as a rat scurried toward a hole. The water, lapping against the posts of the building, created a strange moaning sound.

"Maybe that was what we heard," Katherine whispered doubtfully. "No one seem to be in here."

"I'll not give up the search yet," replied Nancy in a low voice, going into an adjoining room.

"Here! Here!" came a feeble cry.

Giant, eerie shadows leaped at her as she flashed her light into every remote corner of the place. The beam came to rest at last on an old rowboat, half turned against the wall. From its stern protruded a pair of bare feet, bound with a cord.

"There!" cried Katherine in horror. "We find someone!"

Nancy ran to the boat. A glance told her that the limp figure lying across the seat was Mr. Ellington. His hands were bound. A gag in his mouth had slipped a bit, allowing him to make feeble sounds.

"We'll have you out of here in a second," she assured him, as she started to work at the knotted ropes.

Katherine already had removed the gag. "Oh, what have they done to you?" she moaned.

"I was set upon by two men," the artist said hoarsely. "They waylaid my car and brought me here. Since then I've had nothing to eat and only a little water."

"Your torture is over now," Nancy declared,

pulling aside the last rope. "Do you know who they were?"

"No, they wore masks."

"I think I know," Nancy said, trying to hide her rising excitement.

She was staring at Mr. Ellington's bare feet, dangling over the side of the boat.

"They took my shoes and stockings," he apologized. "I—I am ashamed of how I must look."

Nancy paid no heed to the words. "Mr. Ellington! Your left foot!" she exclaimed. "It has a peculiar mark on the sole!"

"Oh, that." The young man tried to draw the foot out of sight. "It was put on when I was a child."

"Then the mark has special significance?" Nancy asked eagerly.

"It was made by a doctor as a means of identifying me," Mr. Ellington explained. "My life story is so fantastic that I never speak of it."

Nancy was about to say more, when Katherine interrupted her. "We must stop talking and help him," she said.

The young man had tried to rise, but now fell back weakly.

"Don't try to move," Nancy said kindly. "I'll take this rope to the boys, so they can tie up your guard, and then they can carry you to the car."

The prisoner was bound, then Ellington was lifted from the boat and removed to his automobile. It was decided that the girls would drive him to his apartment, while the boys turned Cordova over to the police.

When the automobile reached the Inn, Nancy sent Katherine in for a cup of hot soup for Mr. Ellington. The Drew girl hurriedly asked him a few questions. She nodded in satisfaction at his replies.

"Please do not tell Katherine yet," Nancy begged.

"I have something special to ask her before I tell her this," he smiled mysteriously.

All the next day Nancy went from place to place, a smile on her face. Happily she hummed snatches of songs. She was planning a party for her father the following evening.

"And what an unusual party it will be!" she mused. "Oh, I'm so glad Mrs. Alexandra will be well enough to come."

The doctor had said the elderly lady might come to the Drew home directly from the hospital. In view of the fact that she was brooding over her frightful experience with the impostor grandson, he felt the change might benefit her.

"And Mr. Faber found just the right gift for Dad!" Nancy said enthusiastically to Hannah Gruen.

"I'm glad," smiled the housekeeper. "Your father hasn't had a celebration in a long time. He has been working too hard lately, and he'll enjoy this."

By eight o'clock the following evening all of

the invited guests had arrived at the Drew home. Nancy's young friends came in a group, while Mr. Ellington escorted Katherine. She proudly showed Nancy an engagement ring, which she said had belonged to his mother.

"Oh, that's wonderful!" the Drew girl congratulated her.

Mrs. Alexandra and Mr. Faber were among the last to come, the latter bearing a large tissue-wrapped package. Introductions were made, and Mr. Ellington's fine manners greatly impressed the elderly lady.

Then came the surprise of the evening. In a voice vibrant with excitement, Nancy revealed that Mr. Ellington was none other than the real Michael Alexandra.

"This time there can be no mistake," she said to the young man's grandmother. "He has the identifying mark on his foot."

Everyone murmured in surprise. Katherine turned white. Mrs. Alexandra gave a start, but made no sign of being pleased.

"She wants further proof," thought Nancy.

The girl explained that in rescuing the young man from the boathouse she had observed an 'A' shaped marking on his left foot.

"The incision was made by a doctor when I was a child," Mr. Ellington disclosed in a low, musical voice. "I still remember how I howled when that bushy-whiskered old man made the cut."

"What else do you recall?" inquired Mrs. Alexandra, still distant in her manner.

Disillusioned because of her previous mistake, she was afraid to believe yet that Nancy could have found her missing grandson.

"I recall a long hallway with mirrors," Ellington said with a chuckle. "How that place frightened me! Whenever I had to go through it, I would run like a deer."

"It is true, Madame!" whispered Mr. Faber. "He describes the Hall of Mirrors in the palace."

"Come here," Mrs. Alexandra bade the young man. "Let me look into your face. It is true you resemble my son, but you cannot be the long-lost Michael, or you would address me in our native tongue, I'm sure."

Mr. Ellington laughed. Then, to the amazement of the guests, he began to speak to Mrs. Alexandra in words they could not understand. Presently the old lady began to weep, and in a moment clasped him in her arms.

Katherine, who interpreted for the group, assured them that the young man had convinced his grandmother beyond any doubt that he was the true heir. After that everyone seemed to talk at once, and Nancy was asked to explain many things.

She said she had learned of the 'A' shaped incision from a note found in the Footman jewel box. The message had been written by Michael's nurse.

"It said that she was taking the prince to America," the girl disclosed. "The incision was made on the little boy's foot so that there never could be any question of his identity. The faithful woman had left clues in various places, hoping his grandmother would find them upon her return to the palace.

"Only the other day Mrs. Alexandra and I discovered one of them by means of the little nightingale. He was made to sing 'Clue in Jewel Box' by an expert creator of music boxes."

"That man was old Conrad Nicholas, brother-in-law of my nurse, Nada," explained Mr. Ellington. Turning to his newly-found grandmother, he added, "Nada was very, very good to me. She was a mother to me. She died only six months ago, and I have been very sad since then. Not until I met Katherine did I feel happy again, but now that I have a grandmother and a fiancée, I am doubly happy."

"When did Nada write that letter which the impostor used?" George asked. "He said she had died many years before, and the note was dated long ago."

"She wrote it when I was still a little boy, so I would have it in case anything should happen to her," the artist replied. "She gave me the name Francis Baum, so our enemies would not find us. Later I took the name R. H. Ellington as a signature for pictures."

"I like that much better," said his grandmother. "And I do not mind if you keep on using it. I shall never call you Michael, for it will bring up horrible memories of that awful thief."

"After my art portfolio was stolen, I often wondered what became of my little toy lamb," the young man said. "Nada warned me to keep it as extra proof of my identity. I was ashamed to let anyone see me with it, so I kept it in my portfolio."

"It is waiting for you at your new home," smiled the queen mother gaily. "That is, if you will live with me."

After the thrilling reunion of Mrs. Alexandra and her grandson, still another surprise awaited the guests. At a signal from Nancy, Mr. Faber arose to present to Mr. Drew the special birthday gift from his daughter. In a ceremonious speech, the antique dealer declared that it gave him great pleasure to present the "gentleman's box."

"It will become the property of the finest, most unselfish people I have met in this glorious country. Here's to Mr. Drew and his lovely, clever daughter!" he concluded.

There was much hand clapping as Nancy and her father acknowledged the compliment. Everyone crowded close as the package was unwrapped. Mr. Drew lifted out a handsome leather and silver box, its lid embossed with a scene of hunters on horseback. It bore the mark of the skilled silversmith who had created it—Mr. Faber's father.

"This is really fine," Mr. Drew declared, his fingers exploring the intricate work. "I never aspired to own such a distinguished piece."

His words ended in a gasp of astonishment. Somehow the lawyer had pressed a tiny, hidden spring along the side of the "gentleman's box." A false bottom was revealed, and in it was a slip of paper.

"Now what can this be?" inquired Mr. Drew as he scanned the strange figures on the sheet. "This isn't part of the surprise, Mr. Faber?"

"Indeed, it is not," replied the antique dealer. "Until this moment I did not know that the box had a secret opening."

"This seems to be a formula of some sort," Mr. Drew declared after a moment.

"Perhaps the long missing process of enamel making!" cried Mr. Faber. "At one time my father had it in his possession."

Mr. Drew offered the paper to the elderly man, saying, "Then this belongs to you, of course."

Mr. Faber retreated a step. "No! No! The box and its contents are for you and your daughter. I can take back nothing."

"I know what we can do!" laughed Nancy when the matter had reached a deadlock. "Why not form a manufacturing company, comprised of all the persons who helped solve the Clue in the Jewel Box?"

"Now that is an excellent idea," approved

Mr. Faber. "This formula should provide great wealth for any group of persons willing to organize and work."

"Let's make Nancy president," proposed Ned gaily.

Nancy, however, declined the honor.

"I prefer to devote my time to detective work," she declared.

In a short time the girl was to become involved in a strange case, called "The Secret in the Old Attic."

"I'm sure I can do better at solving mysteries than I could at making enamel," Nancy laughed. "I'll turn over the organization task of the new company to Dad, and my share of the profits to his pet charity, the Boys Club!"

THE END